MURDER, SHE WROTE:
A PALETTE FOR MURDER

MURDER, SHE WROTE:
A PALETTE FOR MURDER

Jessica Fletcher & Donald Bain

Based on the Universal television series
created by Peter S. Fischer, Richard
Levinson and William Link

Chivers Press • G.K. Hall & Co.
Bath, England   Thorndike, Maine USA

This Large Print edition is published by Chivers Press, England, and by G.K. Hall & Co., USA.

Published in 2001 in the U.K. by arrangement with Universal.

Published in 2001 in the U.S. by arrangement with Chivers Press Limited.

U.K. Hardcover   ISBN 0-7540-4395-9   (Chivers Large Print)
U.K. Softcover   ISBN 0-7540-4396-7   (Camden Large Print)
U.S. Softcover   ISBN 0-7838-9319-1   (Nightingale Series Edition)

The text of this Large Print edition is unabridged.
Other aspects of the book may vary from the original edition.

Set in 16 pt. New Times Roman.

Printed in Great Britain on acid-free paper.

British Library Cataloguing in Publication Data available

Library of Congress Cataloging-in-Publication Data

Bain, Donald, 1935–
    A palette for murder : a murder, she wrote mystery : a novel / by Jessica Fletcher and Donald Bain ; based on the Universal television series created by Peter S. Fischer, Richard Levinson & William Link.
      p.   cm.
    ISBN 0-7838-9319-1 (lg. print : sc : alk. paper)
    1. Fletcher, Jessica (Fictitious character)—Fiction. 2. Women novelists—Fiction. 3. Artists' models—Fiction. 4. Large type books. I. Title.
PS3552.A376 P35 2001
813'.54—dc21
                             00–049884

IN MEMORY OF

Jack Pearl
Jack Douglas
Long John Nebel
Hank Caruthers
and
R. H. 'Red' Sutherland

CHAPTER ONE

'Why does it matter?'

'It matters because good writing always matters,' I said, allowing an involuntary sigh of frustration to escape my lips. 'I care about good writing because I am a professional. Readers care about good writing. They expect, and deserve it. That, sir, is why it matters.'

My mini-sermon was met with a vacant stare from the student who'd challenged my criticism of his short story. It was mid-June, and I was teaching a group of young aspiring writers at New York University. Since starting to give these occasional workshops a few years ago, they'd become a regular part of my yearly schedule. I loved doing it—I've reached an age where I try to do only things I enjoy—but it could be frustrating at times. This was one of those moments.

My stubborn student was a young man wearing a baseball hat backward. He'd been a thorn in my side for the entire three days, mostly because he talked a better game than he wrote.

He made it obvious on the first day that he considered the writing of murder mystery novels to be a subspecies of literature, beneath his dignity. The first time he cast a disparaging remark about the genre, I asked why, if he felt that way, he was taking my seminar. His reply: 'I may want to turn to writing mysteries if I ever get hard up for money.'

I allowed this and other snide comments to slide, but must admit that by this, the third day, my patience was running thin.

'I think it says exactly what I wanted it to say,' he said, referring to the paragraph on which I'd zeroed in.

'Well, Richard, then allow me to read it again aloud. I shall do so very slowly in the hope that you get the point.' I picked up the page on which the paragraph in question was contained and read: ' "The first thing she noticed upon entering the living room was a large, circular bloodstain in the rug that was in the center." '

I looked at him.

He shrugged.

'Richard, the way you structured this sentence, the reader doesn't know whether the bloodstain was in the center of the rug, or the rug was in the center of the room. That ambiguity would be cleared up if it read, "The first thing she noticed upon entering the living room was a large, circular bloodstain in the center of the rug." '

He guffawed and looked to his fellow students for support. I was pleased to see he received none.

'I still don't see why—'

I dropped his paper, picked up another, and

began to read from it. I'd had enough of Richard, with his silly-looking hat and arrogant attitude.

The rest of the morning went well, Richard the duly noted exception. Most of the students in the class had been attentive and responsive to my suggestions, and some had brought in copies of my books for me to sign, which I happily did.

I checked the clock on the wall: twelve-thirty. Time for a quick lunch with the dean of NYU's writing program, and then, hopefully, a quick ride on the jitney to the Hamptons, where I planned to spend the next ten days relaxing after a demanding, frustrating spring.

*　　　*　　　*

I'd run into problems with my most recent manuscript. Instead of delivering it by March to my publisher, Vaughan Buckley of Buckley House, I didn't put the finishing touches on it until a week before coming to New York to teach. Vaughan was characteristically gracious about my lateness, but I wasn't pleased with it. I pride myself on meeting deadlines, and have little patience with writers who don't share that attitude.

'Sorry for the delay,' I'd said after delivering the manuscript four days ago, and after one of his secretaries had served me tea in Vaughan's spacious, handsomely appointed office. 'I had to rewrite the final third to make it work.'

'No problem,' he said. 'I'm sure the delay has resulted in an even better book. So, you're about to teach another seminar.'

'Yes. And then off to your beloved Hamptons.'

'It's going to be wonderful having you out there with us, Jess. I apologize again for the timing. If Olga and I had known you planned to take some vacation time after teaching, we wouldn't have started a major renovation on the house.'

'Don't give it another thought.'

Vaughan and Olga Buckley, two of my favorite people in the world, have a summer home in the Hamptons. I'd never seen it, but they'd shown me photographs. It was lovely, situated right on the water, with graceful porches affording magnificent views in every direction.

I had mixed emotions, in a sense, about not being able to stay with these dear friends. On the one hand, I always enjoy their company and revel in their fawning over me. Vaughan and Olga Buckley are the perfect host and hostess.

On the other hand, there is something appealing to me about being on my own. Being a houseguest carries with it certain obligations and restrictions.

Actually, the situation in the Hamptons represented the best of both worlds. I would be staying at a lovely inn, chosen by the Buckleys, but would be within minutes of their home. Having it both ways.

Vaughan escorted me to the elevator. 'Teach good, Jess,' he said. 'Don't let those kids put anything over on you.'

'You bet I won't.'

'And be on the lookout for the next Agatha Christie—or J.D. Fletcher.'

'I'll do that. Thanks again, Vaughan, for understanding the late delivery of the manuscript. See you in the Hamptons in a few days.'

'Right you are, Jess. And don't worry about your luggage. I'll have it picked up at your hotel the last day of your stay. It'll be at the inn when you arrive.'

*   *   *

My classroom cleared out. The last student to leave was Richard, who approached me as I was packing my briefcase. 'If I decide to write a murder mystery, Mrs Fletcher, can I send it to you to read?'

The gall, I thought. I smiled. 'Of course, Richard. It was a pleasure having you in class.'

Lunch in the faculty dining room was low-calorie and pleasant. The dean, a bear of a man with white hair, thick, unruly black eyebrows and a Santa Clause twinkle in his eye, said, 'The feedback on your seminar every year, Jessica, is always top-notch. We're truly grateful to have you share your experience and talent with us.'

'The pleasure is all mine, Dean Carlisle. My fondest wish is that one of my students will go on to write the Great American Novel, and win all sorts of awards for it.'

'And be paid handsomely as well.'

'Yes. That, too.'

'So you're off to the Hamptons,' he said as he walked me from the building to the street.

'Yes. I've never been there.'

'I thought every writer ended up in the Hamptons—much to the chagrin of some.'

'Well, I don't intend to rub elbows with other writers. I've had enough of writing to last me a few months. This is strictly relaxation, Dean Carlisle. A needed case of R and R.'

'Well, you enjoy it. Say hello to Vaughan Buckley for me. See you in six months?'

'You can count on it.'

Now alone—alone in the sense that no one was with *me*; the West Village was teeming with tourists, students, and other assorted New Yorkers—I looked across the street to the famed Washington Arch, which marks the beginning of Fifth Avenue, and stands as a landmark to Washington Square, the busy park surrounding it. I waited for a break in the traffic, then crossed and entered the square. two statues of George Washington defined the east and west boundaries. *Washington as*

6

President is on the west pier of the arch, *Washington as Commander-in-Chief* anchors the east pier.

I checked my watch. I had time to kill before catching the Hampton Jitney at Eighty-sixth Street, on the Upper East Side, one of many stops it makes along Lexington Avenue. A short stroll through Washington Square was in order. It was a lovely day, spring warmth in the air, sun shining brightly, the blue sky a scrim for puffs of fast-moving white clouds. Because Vaughan had my luggage picked up at the hotel that morning, I only had to carry my shoulder bag, and a large black leather portfolio that didn't weigh much.

I hadn't gone very far when I was stopped by a scraggly young man. He pulled his hand from the pocket of his ragged jacket and held it out to me. In his palm were two small glassine packets. 'The best stuff, lady. Top of the line.'

My first reaction was to yell for the police. He was obviously offering me illegal drugs. But I decided it would be fruitless. I turned and walked with purpose in another direction. Frankly, I was surprised at being offered drugs in Washington Square. New York City's government had taken aggressive steps to clean up the park, and had been largely successful, as far as I knew. The last time I was there—six months ago when I taught a previous seminar at NYU—a friend had met

7

me for lunch. As we walked through the square she had said, 'It's so nice to have the park reclaimed from the drug dealers. Sort of like going back to when Henry James was writing about it.'

'It can be done if people put their minds to it,' I said.

'This used to be a hanging gallows,' she said, pointing to a giant elm tree, the oldest in the city. 'And this was the original potter's field.'

'I almost wish you hadn't mentioned it,' I said. 'The contemplation of people hanging from that tree isn't very pretty.'

'There are some people I wouldn't mind seeing swinging from its branches,' she said. 'I'm sure you have a few, too.'

'None I can think of at the moment,' I replied, and changed the subject.

The image of people being hanged in Washington Square has been with me ever since that conversation. But I dismissed it from my mind this day, hailed a passing cab, and headed uptown, instructing the driver to let me off at Second Avenue at Eighty-fourth Street. There's a shop there, Oldies, Goldies, and Moldies, that I was told carried a wonderful variety of clocks. My friend back home in Cabot Cove, Dr. Seth Hazlitt, had mentioned to me before I left that he was looking for a certain type of clock. If this shop had it, I wanted to buy it for him.

I'd no sooner paid the driver—a rough,

8

grizzled sort of fellow—and stepped out of his cab when a car bumped into the back of it. It was the mildest of collisions; I didn't see any damage. But both drivers leaped out and started screaming at each other. This led to a fistfight. And then, to my horror, my cab-driver pulled a lead pipe from beneath his seat and hit the other driver in the head with it.

I turned away just before the moment of bloody impact and walked quickly down the street. Two uniformed policemen who'd witnessed it ran past me in the direction of the confrontation. What senseless brutality over something so minor, I thought as I kept walking until reaching Third Avenue. The heck with looking for a clock. I wasn't about to go back to the scene of the violence.

As I waited for the light to change, I noticed a folding table to my right on which books were displayed. I went to it and scanned the many titles for sale. Most were children's books. But on one end was a pile of paperback books without their covers. I looked closer. On the pile were a few copies of one of my novels, published in paperback a year ago. The man was selling them for fifty cents.

Well, I'll be, I thought as I picked up one of the books and thumbed through it. I'd heard of the illegal practice by some bookstores and distributors of tearing covers from paperback books, then sending the covers back to the publisher for a refund and selling the stripped books themselves. Book publishing is one of the last industries in America in which the product is sold on consignment. A bookstore might order twenty paperback copies of a certain book. If it sells five, it need only tear off the fifteen covers of the remaining ones and send them back for full credit. The expectation, of course, is that the books themselves will be destroyed.

But there is an obvious black market in coverless paperbacks, and here was the first example I'd personally experienced.

'You want?' the man behind the table asked.

I dropped my book on the pile and shook my head. 'No, no thank you. Have a nice day.'

By the time I settled in a window seat on the large, comfortable and modern touring bus— calling it a jitney is misleading—and had accepted the attendant's offer of orange juice and a bag of peanuts, I was more than ready to leave what is affectionately called The Big Apple.

My pompous student, Richard, had annoyed me with his arrogant views on writing.

I'd been offered illicit drugs in Washington Square.

I'd seen a man attempt to beat another man's brains out with a lead pipe, all because their respective automobiles touched.

And now copies of one of my books were being illegally sold on the streets of Manhattan.

10

I couldn't wait to get to the idyllic Hamptons. I'd had enough crime to last me a good long time.

CHAPTER TWO

The Hampton Jitney was full, and I was glad I'd made my reservation well in advance. Because I had a window seat, I had to excuse myself to the young man seated on the aisle. He, too, had a large portfolio similar to mine.

'Hi,' he said after I'd settled in.

'Hi,' I said.

'I haven't seen you before.'

Why would not seeing me before strike him as being unusual? I wondered. 'Do you mean on this jitney?' I asked.

His grin broadened. 'Yeah,' he said. 'I take it all the time. Most people take it regularly.'

'I didn't realize that,' I said. 'This is my first trip.'

His smile faded and his brow knitted. 'Do I know you from someplace?' he asked. 'I mean, someplace other than the jitney.'

'I really wouldn't know.'

'Are you a famous artist?'

I laughed. 'Goodness, no. I can't even draw the proverbial straight line.'

His eyes went to my portfolio. 'I figured you were an artist because of that,' he said, pointing to it.

'Oh that,' I said. 'Just to carry some oversize
... *things*.'

My seat companion started talking to the
person across the aisle, giving me the
opportunity to open one of two books I'd
brought with me to read on vacation. But I had
trouble starting it. There was too much to see
out my window.

The driver left Manhattan via the Queens
Midtown Tunnel and headed east on the Long
Island Expressway. Although it wasn't rush
hour, at least according to my definition,
traffic was horrendous and stayed that way
until we'd reached Suffolk County, where
things opened up and we were able to make
better time. Soon, we were on smaller local
roads, rolling along through farmland and
passing lovely older homes mingled with more
modern structures featuring lots of glass and
natural woods.

I enjoyed my solitude, shifting my attention
between the book and the scenery. But
eventually, my seat companion struck up
another conversation with me. 'I still think I
know you from somewhere,' he said. 'By the
way, name's Chris Turi.' He extended his
hand.

'Pleased to meet you,' I said.

'And you are?'

'J. D. Fletcher,' I mumbled.

'Fletcher. Fletcher. The mystery writer?'

I leaned close to him. 'Yes, but I would just as soon not broadcast it. I'm coming to the Hamptons for what I hope is a very quiet ten days away from anything having to do with writing.'

He smiled. 'Sure. I understand.'

'You thought I was an artist because of this portfolio I'm carrying,' I said. 'I see you're carrying one, too. Are you an artist?'

He nodded enthusiastically. 'A struggling one,' he said. 'Maybe someday my name will be as famous as yours.'

'I certainly hope so,' I said, not sure whether that indicated a certain pomposity on my part. 'What sort of art do you do?'

'Hard to categorize,' he replied. 'Modern, I guess, although I've been trying to incorporate a more traditional approach to some of my works.'

'Combining the old masters with modern design?' I asked, hoping my question didn't sound stupid.

'Something like that,' he said.

We didn't have time to discuss it further because minutes later, our driver pulled to the curb in the center of the charming Hamptons village that would be my home for the next ten days. Mr. Turi and I shook hands: 'I'll probably see you around,' he said. 'Not a very big place.'

'Well, if we do bump into each other, I'd enjoy seeing some of your work.'

'Sure. Be my pleasure. Want to see some now?'

I saw Vaughan and Olga Buckley waiting for me on the sidewalk, their two little dogs, Sadie and Rose, on leashes. 'Sorry, but there's no time,' I said. 'Maybe I'll see you in a restaurant or café.'

'Yeah. That would be good. Nice meeting you, Mrs. Fletcher.'

'Same here.'

'Jessica, how wonderful to see you,' Olga Buckley said, handing the leashes to Vaughan and giving me a hug.

'And good to see you again, Olga. You look stunning as usual.' Olga Buckley had once been a top fashion model in Manhattan. When she married the dashing young publisher, Vaughan Buckley, news of their permanent liaison was big news on the society pages. Although her modeling career ended a number of years ago, she looked as good today as when her cameo face and slender figure graced the covers of some of America's leading fashion magazines.

Vaughan, who loved clothes and was always impeccably dressed, was no exception this day. He wore gray slacks with a razor crease, a double-breasted blue blazer with gold buttons, and a red-and-white checkered button-down shirt open at the collar. A red handkerchief jauntily protruded from his breast pocket. He kissed me on the cheek. Sadie and Rose yapped at my feet; I crouched and gave them each a scratch behind the ears.

'Well,' I said, straightening up, 'here I am. What a charming village.'

'That it is,' Vaughan said. 'Of course, it'll get too crowded now that the season is upon us. But that adds a certain vitality to it.'

As we slowly walked along the street in the direction of the inn they'd chosen for me, Vaughan said, 'Olga and I are still considering buying some property up in Cabot Cove.'

Olga laughed. 'Ever since Vaughan came back from visiting you there, all he's talked about is how beautiful Cabot Cove is, and how much we'd enjoy having a getaway there. He says a friend of yours makes the best blueberry pancakes he's ever tasted.'

'That would be Mara. Everything she cooks is good.'

The inn was located on the main street, set back from the sidewalk. It was lovely in a gingerbread way, gray shingles and immaculately painted white trim cut into a series of circles that bordered the top and sides of the door. A pair of white wicker rockers stood on a small front porch. A bicycle rack holding a half-dozen bikes was to the right of the porch.

'It looks lovely,' I said.

'We think you'll enjoy staying here, Jessica,' Olga said. 'Dreadful timing, having our house renovated just when you come to visit. But this

15

inn is really very comfortable. It only has a few rooms, but one is a suite in the back, overlooking a lovely garden. That's your room.'

'Sounds yummy,' I said.

The Buckleys were greeted warmly by the inn's owner, an older, cherubic gentleman with a baldpate, and a fringe of white hair that looked like cotton pasted to his temples. His name was Joseph Scott, and he seemed genuinely enthusiastic about my being a guest. He ushered us into a small sitting room with door-to-ceiling bookcases on one wall. With great pride, he pointed to a section that contained, at least it looked to me, every book I'd ever written. 'My personal J. D. Fletcher library,' he announced.

'I'm very flattered, Mr. Scott. I don't know of anyone who has *every* book I've written.'

'My hope is that you'll sign them all for me,' he said. 'That is, if it wouldn't be too much of an imposition.'

I took in the room with a sweep of my hand and said, 'I think I'll be spending many hours here, plenty of time to sign your books a dozen times each.'

'Splendid,' he said, rubbing his hands. 'I'm sure you're tired after your trip, Mrs. Fletcher. Let me show you your suite.'

The suite at the rear of the house was as tastefully decorated and furnished as the downstairs. Everything was the color of ripe

16

peaches, accented with dazzling white trim. The king-size iron-and-brass bed was covered with a lacy, crocheted spread. A magnificent painted leather screen stood next to a large fireplace. An ancient, lovingly restored armoire that must have had to have been disassembled to fit it into the room, dominated the wall. The bathroom was charming: a footed tub, pedestal sink, gleaming hardwood floor, and needlepoint rug.

My luggage rested on a chest at the foot of the bed. I leaned my oversize black portfolio against it. 'What have we here?' Vaughan asked, touching it.

'What?' I asked.

'This artist's portfolio. You aren't thinking of abandoning writing for a career in art, are you?'

I hoped my forced laughter wasn't obvious. 'Just some—oversize—*things*,' I said.

Seemingly satisfied with my response, Vaughan went to the windows spanning the back wall and pulled the frilly white curtains aside. The rear of the property had the peaceful look of a classic English country garden.

'I think I'm going to be blissfully happy here,' I announced.

'And that's all we want for you, Jessica,' Olga said, giving my arm a squeeze. 'Why don't you freshen up, maybe take a nap. We are having dinner together?'

'Looking forward to it,' I said. 'And yes, I'd like to get unpacked, freshen up, and maybe close my eyes for twenty minutes. Where are we having dinner?'

'Della Femina, in East Hampton.'

'The famous advertising man?' I asked.

'One and the same,' Olga said. 'He opened his restaurant here in 1991, and it's been a success ever since. No matter what you order, save room for the warm *valrhona* chocolate cake. Served with fresh raspberries and chocolate-hazelnut gelato. To die for.'

'I was determined not to—'

'No diets this trip, Jess,' said Vaughan. 'Great story about Jerry Della Femina. Years ago he was pitching a possible Japanese client for his agency. He became frustrated during the meeting and said, "How about we launch a campaign with the theme, 'From Those Wonderful Folks Who Brought You Pearl Harbor'?"'

'Did he get the account?' I asked.

'No. But he wrote a best-selling book with that title.'

'And now he owns a restaurant.'

'And a good one,' Vaughan said. 'Let's go, Olga, let the lady relax. We'll be by to pick you up at seven.'

'I'll be waiting.'

Once the Buckleys were gone, Mr. Scott asked whether I'd like tea.

'As a matter of fact, I would,' I said.

18

During his absence, I unpacked and put my clothing away. I waited until he'd delivered the tea and left the room before opening the art portfolio I'd been carrying. A lovely waning light spilled through the suite's windows, and I held each item from the portfolio up to it. Some of them made me smile. Others caused me to wince. There were four watercolor landscapes, only one of which captured the scene with any validity. Pencil sketches of faces and figures were mostly out-of-proportion—a nose too broad, ears not matching facial structure, arms not in true relationship to the body. I responded favorably to one still life of a bowl of fruit. 'Not bad,' I said aloud.

There was a knock at the door.

I quickly put the drawings and paintings back in the portfolio, and answered. It was Mr. Scott. 'Sorry to bother you, Mrs. Fletcher, but I just thought you might like this selection of our local newspapers and tourist magazines.'

'Thank you so much,' I said. 'I would like to read up a little on the area before venturing out. This is my first visit to the Hamptons.'

'I'll do everything possible to make it memorable,' he said, backing out of the room and closing the door behind him.

Unpacked and freshened up, I decided not to nap but to take a walk before dinner. I stopped on my way out of the inn to admire some of the art on the walls of the common areas, and the antique furniture gracing each room. Filled with a sense of well-being, I stepped out onto the main street. Night hadn't fallen yet, but wasn't far away.

I went to my right because there seemed to be more shops in that direction. Turning to the left would have taken me out of town into what appeared to be a residential area.

I paused in front of store windows and admired the attractive display of goods— jewelry, rare books, perfumes, and toiletries, the sort of merchandise one expects to find in a resort town.

At the corner was an art gallery. There was a lot of activity inside, so I went in and was greeted by a middle-aged man wearing an obviously expensive blue suit of English cut. 'Good evening,' he said.

'Good evening. What a lovely gallery. It's larger than one imagines from outside.'

'Never large enough. Are you interested in something of Joshua's specifically, or just perusing?'

'Perusing, I suppose. Joshua?'

His expression said to me that I had said something remarkably inept. 'Joshua Leopold,' he said.

I looked at the art on the nearest wall. 'Is he the artist?'

His expression deepened; I guess I was asking dumber questions all the time. 'Joshua Leopold is perhaps the most highly regarded young artist in the field today. We're his exclusive representatives in the Hamptons. Our sister gallery in Manhattan also features his work.'

'Well, I'm impressed,' I said, not really meaning it. The man's pomposity was off-putting, but I decided to not let that deter me. 'I think I'll—peruse, if you don't mind.'

'Of course. Just summon me if you need anything. I am at your disposal. My name is Maurice St. James.'

I didn't bother to introduce myself, and slowly walked the perimeter of the gallery. Mr. Leopold, the artist, certainly had a strong style, working with large areas of vivid color that seemed to have been randomly applied to the canvas. I thought of Jackson Pollock, who influenced an entire generation of artists working in what some critic termed 'Action Painting.' It's never been my cup of tea. I'm a traditionalist in most things, including painting.

But I could see the appeal of this young artist's work. It hit me between the eyes, the colors swirling in front of me like a runaway kaleidoscope. I've never claimed to be an expert in judging art. But I like to think I have as much appreciation of the visual as the next person. The problem comes in evaluating the open-market value of an unknown artist's works. I would not have bought any of the art hanging on the gallery's walls. Well, perhaps a hundred dollars for a few of the pieces that caught my eye, particularly the only work that had some roots in realism. By standing back and squinting, I discerned through the maze of yellows, reds, and purples a nude woman, sitting on what might have been a toadstool, her head down between her knees. At least that's what it appeared to me to be.

I continued browsing before consulting a leatherbound book containing descriptions of Mr. Leopold's art, and the prices for it. I was shocked. Some of his smaller pieces were offered at ten thousand dollars. Others were triple that. The one depicting the naked young woman—if my judgment of its subject matter was accurate—was one hundred thousand dollars. At least I'd picked what others considered the most valuable of the collection.

As I headed for the door, Mr. St. James stepped into my path. 'See anything that tickles your fancy?'

'All of it,' I said. 'I'll take all of it.'

It was nice to see this self-assured gentleman at a loss for words. It didn't last long. He smiled and said, 'In that case, I am sure a substantial discount will be in order.'

'Yes, I'm sure it will be,' I said. 'Decide how much the lot will cost. I'll come back tomorrow.'

I left him slack-jawed. When I got to the sidewalk and was out of his view, I started to giggle. 'What fun,' I said to myself, retracing my steps to the inn. What a wonderful fantasy, to imagine buying an entire gallery's collection of an up-and-coming artist. Of course, I had no intention of going back, and quickly put the episode out of mind by the time Vaughan and Olga greeted me in the lobby of Scott's Inn.

'Took a walk?' Olga asked.

'Yes. A very pretty village.'

'We knew you'd like it,' said Vaughan.

'Buy anything?' asked Olga.

'Oh, no. But maybe tomorrow. Ready to go? I'm famished.'

CHAPTER THREE

'Is that—?'

Vaughan Buckley smiled. 'Yes, it's Barbra Streisand.'

I looked to my left. 'Isn't that—?'

A larger smile from Vaughan. 'Right again. John Kennedy, Jr.,' who was with a beautiful young woman.

I've never considered myself to be unduly starstruck. But there were so many recognizable faces in Della Femina, I was in danger of losing my aloof attitude toward the rich and famous.

The restaurant was everything Vaughan and Olga had said it would be. The dining room had a quiet elegance, although the bar area was considerably lighter in decor and spirit.

We were seated at a choice corner table set for six.

'Are others joining us?' I asked after a waiter had taken drink orders.

'Yes,' Vaughan replied. 'There are some people we thought you'd enjoy meeting.'

'Not writers, I hope.'

'No fear,' said Olga. 'We're being joined by friends from the art world.'

'Anyone I'd know?' I asked.

'Probably not,' said Vaughan, 'unless you follow the art scene very closely. One of the reasons for the major renovation of our house out here is to create more wall space for some art we've recently collected.'

Olga chimed in: 'Every place we've lived has always been dominated by wall-to-wall bookcases, overflowing with books. We decided to shift emphasis and surround ourselves with more visual things.'

'So have I,' I said, 'although not on the scale you're talking about. I've been buying works by Maine artists, and have the same problem, finding the right wall space to properly display them.'

Comparing our relative lack of wall space was interrupted by the arrival of two other guests, Jacob and Alix Simmons. Once they were seated and introductions had been made, Vaughan said, 'Jake and Alix are artist representatives in the city.'

'That must be fascinating,' I said.

'Probably not nearly as interesting as writing bestselling murder mysteries read by millions of people,' Jake Simmons said. He was a short, slender man, with a deeply tanned, finely chiseled face and prominent hooked nose. His wife, Alix—interesting name, I thought; I mentally file interesting names for use in future books—was considerably heavier than her husband, although not overweight, a boxy, square body sheathed in a simple black dress, her oval face smooth and pale compared to her husband's copper tan.

'Having millions of people read my books is fun,' I said. 'Writing them is—well, I don't find it to be fun very often. Do you represent any artists I would know?'

Alix replied, 'Probably. We're partial to older, more conventional artists.'

I wasn't sure whether I should take offense at her assumption that age would dictate my preferences in art, so I didn't. She named a few people she and Jake represented, none of whom registered with me.

'I must admit,' I said, 'that I'm not well versed and educated in art, or artists.'

'What a refreshing candor,' Alix said. 'Most people try to impress us with knowledge they claim to have about art—but don't.'

'I was in a gallery earlier today,' I said. 'Right up the street from the inn.'

'Oh? Which one?' Vaughan asked.

'I don't know the name of it, but it features

the work of—'

A tall, heavyset man came to the table.

'Hans,' Vaughan said, standing and shaking the recent arrival's beefy hand. 'You know Jake and Alix. Say hello to Jessica Fletcher.'

I extended my hand from where I sat. The big man took it in both of his and seemed to massage it, saying in a deep, hoarse voice, his accent testifying to his German heritage, 'The famous writer. Ah, yes. What a pleasure. I am Hans Muller, Mrs. Fletcher.'

He let go of my hand, sat in the remaining empty chair, and lighted a cigarette. I was surprised; no one else at the table smoked. But because there was an ashtray, I assumed we'd been seated in the smoking section of the restaurant. Was it because Vaughan knew Mr. Muller smoked, and wanted to accommodate him? That unspoken question was immediately answered by Muller: 'I trust you'll be tolerant of this man's only remaining vice, Mrs. Fletcher. These good, healthy people always are.'

'Hans is German,' Olga said. 'They smoke a lot.'

Muller laughed and lighted another. 'Mrs. Buckley is correct, as usual,' he said. 'We did away with the Nazis after the war. The American *health* Nazis haven't managed to gain a foothold in Germany.'

I wondered whether the debate about Muller's smoking might turn nasty, but was

26

relieved when the subject was dropped, and conversation turned to other things, with Muller piling up a mountain of cigarette butts in the ashtray.

I followed the Buckleys' recommendation when ordering dinner: A huge, peppery *Portobello* mushroom as an appetizer, a perfectly cooked blackened tuna steak, and rolls from famed Zabar's in Manhattan that rivaled Charlene Sassi's baking back home. The conversation was spirited and friendly, most of it a discussion of the art world that was for me, at once, interesting yet obscure. Muller, on his second pack of cigarettes, said, 'I stopped in to see Maurice on my way here.'

At first, I didn't connect the name with the gentleman who'd greeted me at the gallery featuring the works of Joshua Leopold. Realizing I was out of the loop, Vaughan Buckley said, 'Maurice St. James owns a gallery just down the street from where you're staying, Jessica. He features an artist named Joshua Leopold.'

'Oh, of course,' I said. 'I—'

Muller laughed, causing him to cough. 'A wonderful story from Maurice,' he said. 'A woman came into the gallery this evening and offered to buy every piece in the place.'

'All of it?' Olga Buckley said, her eyes wide. 'Who was she?'

'All of it,' said Muller. 'Maurice didn't get her name. He said she looked vaguely familiar, but doesn't know why. She's coming back tomorrow with an offer.'

'Maurice must be in heaven,' Alix Simmons said.

'A shame Leopold isn't around to enjoy it,' said Jacob Simmons.

'Yes, that's true,' Muller said.

The banter ceased, and they all looked at me.

'She must be—very rich,' I said.

'Must be,' they agreed.

'You said it's a shame the artist isn't around to enjoy it.'

'Unfortunate, but true,' Muller said. 'He died earlier this year.'

'How old was he?' I asked.

'Thirty-one,' Vaughan said.

'Thirty-two,' Muller corrected.

'Hans is an expert on Joshua Leopold,' Olga explained. 'He has a large Leopold collection back in Germany.'

Muller smiled at me, and I noticed for the first time how yellow his teeth were, and that a tooth was missing on each side. 'Our generation's Picasso,' he said. 'Pollock.'

'How impressive,' I said. 'How did Mr. Leopold die?'

Alix Simmons replied, 'A frightfully premature heart attack.'

'So young,' I said.

'And so much more art to create,' said Muller.

'I can see why this mystery woman wants to buy up everything of his she can.'

'That's what you need, Hans,' Vaughan said, laughing. 'To hook up with a filthy rich woman who wants to buy Joshua Leopolds for you.'

Muller placed his hands over his heart and rolled his eyes up. 'Every man's dream,' he said. 'A woman of beauty and wealth, who loves Leopold as much as I do.'

Although the dinner left me little room for dessert, I was compelled to try the *valrhona* chocolate cake.

Olga hadn't overstated its beauty and taste. It was heavenly.

Everyone ordered after-dinner drinks except me. I glanced at Hans Muller, who was drunk, I judged, and very tired. Large, watery eyes had lowered to half-mast, and his speech had become sloppy. He looked at his watch. 'Damn jet lag,' he said. 'Ten o'clock here. Let me see. That makes it—it makes it four tomorrow morning for me.'

'Still in the habit of never changing your watch when you travel?' Vaughan said.

'Ya. I always keep it on Germany time, and translate.'

'So do I,' I said. 'Not Germany time. But I always keep it set to Cabot Cove time no matter where I am.'

'Cabot Cove—?'

'Where I'm from,' I said. 'This has been a lovely evening, but I'm afraid I'm suffering a little jet lag myself. Hampton Jitney lag is more like it, I suppose.'

'This has been a nice evening,' Olga said as we made our way to the door. 'Breakfast at nine? Our house? They haven't demolished the kitchen yet.'

'Oh, Olga, I would love to but—'

She and her husband looked at me.

'I have a—I have a—a need to walk a beach at sunrise. Yes, that's it. I promised myself to spend each morning meditating. Besides, after this huge dinner, the thought of putting anything else in my stomach is too formidable. Lunch? Can we catch up for lunch at some pretty little café? My treat.'

'All right,' Vaughan said. 'I'll call you at Scott's Inn—after you're done meditating and communing with the sandpipers.'

I hated to lie to them, but I couldn't bring myself to admit what I really had planned for the following morning. Maybe one day I'd get over my reluctance to bare my soul, and admit to giving vent to a secret and powerful passion.

In the meantime, a few white lies would have to be tolerated.

CHAPTER FOUR

The naked young man slowly climbed down from the low platform on which he'd been posing, picked up a white terry cloth robe at his feet, put it on, and headed for a table on which a large coffee urn and a platter of doughnuts were displayed.

'You're getting chubby, Willard,' the instructor told the model. 'Time for Weight Watchers.'

The model, who hadn't cracked a smile for the entire one-hour session, glared at the instructor, dropped a doughnut back onto the tray, and left the room.

The fifteen students drifted in the direction of the refreshments. As they did, the instructor, Carlton Wells, wandered among the easels, stopping at each to check on each artist's progress. His expressive face was easy to read: a frown, a smile, a puzzled look, downright disgust.

As I stood in line for coffee, I glanced over my shoulder to check his reaction to my sketch. It was noncommittal. Better than disgust, I thought.

'How can you sketch wearing those big dark glasses?' a young woman asked me after I'd drawn my coffee and was sipping it in a corner.

'These? Oh, I have an—an eye infection. Actually, I can see just fine.'

Her eyes traveled up to the red turban I wore.

'A hair infection,' I said with a smile.

She went to where a knot of younger artists congregated. No question about it; I was hands

31

down the oldest student in the studio. Which didn't bother me. I'd gotten over worrying about my age the day I decided almost two years ago to give vent to what had been a secret passion for a long time, the urge to paint.

Was I too old to take up a new hobby, to learn a new and different art?

I decided that I was not too old, and took my first tentative steps to becoming a visual artist. I didn't expect miracles, nor did I envision myself painting anything good enough to be of interest to anyone but me. But that would be good enough.

My first step was to buy a few books on art and some basic supplies. I had no idea what kind of art I wished to create. I would stand in museums marveling at the great works on the walls, including one entire day of Washington's magnificent National Gallery of Art, where I reveled in the splendor and indescribable talent of Botticelli and da Vinci, Raphael and Van Dyck, Cézanne and Monet and Renoir and van Gogh.

But while they were inspirational, they did not inspire in me any foolish notion of trying to achieve their artistic level.

So I lowered my sights and spent more time studying contemporary artists, not those who pour paint on large canvases, or wrap objects in plastic and call it art, but to younger artists who have learned their craft, and apply it to their creative visions.

Although I'd decided to pursue the study of art, I was never able to shake a certain embarrassment about it. Silly, I knew. But there is something daunting about creating a drawing or painting, and then having someone else view it. I don't feel that way about the books I write. Maybe that's because I've been writing for a very long time, and am comfortable with the process.

But there was another reason for my reticence about admitting to having taken up art, or allowing others to witness the results.

When people read my books, it takes them time to get through all the pages.

Reaction to a painting or drawing is immediate.

The instructor, Carlton Wells, came up behind me. 'Not bad,' he said.

'What? Oh, my sketch. I don't think it's very—'

'No false modesty, Mrs. Fechter. It's looking good.'

'Thank you.'

I'd registered for the class under an assumed name. I suppose I could have chosen a pseudonym farther afield from my own, but hadn't thought fast enough.

'I'll be interested in how you handle the next model.'

'I hope to your satisfaction, Mr. Wells.'

'Carlton. Call me Carlton.'

'All right—Carlton.'

Carlton was a middle-aged man wanting desperately to be twenty years younger. He wore his graying hair long in the back, secured by what looked to me to be a silver and turquoise clip of Zuni origin. He was bare-chested beneath a brown corduroy jacket that was, to be kind, well-worn. His jeans had holes at the knees, although I suspected he'd cut them, rather than having it occur naturally through wear and age. The jeans looked new. Leather sandals on surprisingly large bare feet completed the 'look.'

I've always been more comfortable with people who simply get dressed in the morning, rather than costuming themselves. But I didn't let that cloud my judgment of Carlton, who'd been pleasant and courteous to me and the others in the class.

Ten minutes later, we were all behind our easels awaiting the next model. She came through a door behind the refreshments table wearing what appeared to be the same white robe worn by our male model. She lazily ascended the platform, tossed the robe to the floor, and stood naked before us. There wasn't a hint, an expression, a gesture to indicate that she was uneasy being nude in front of fifteen strangers, male and female.

She was a pretty young girl, in her early twenties I judged, but not beautiful. At least not according to the prevailing standards set

34

by the pundits of beauty in Hollywood, or the modeling agencies. Her features were too coarse to be labeled classic. Sensuous, though, large brown heavy-lidded eyes, lips full and fleshy, thick, auburn hair obviously washed that morning and catching the sun that poured through large windows on the studio's north wall.

Her body was firm and without blemish, breasts in proportion to her overall frame. I judged her to be only slightly over five feet tall, certainly nothing willowy about her. She had sturdy, healthy legs that undoubtedly served her well in a gym, or when playing volleyball on a beach.

'Well, let's begin,' Wells said.

I noticed that the model, who was introduced to us as Miki, wore white sweat socks, her only clothing. I felt a chill, and checked her for goose bumps. None. She evidently was used to being naked in cold rooms.

'All right, my budding Rembrandts and Caravaggios, pick up your pencils and go to work.' To Miki: 'Ten minutes, my dear. Profile. Sit up straight. Hair out of your eyes. That's it. A little to the left. Aha. Perfect. Hold that pose.'

I glanced over at the easel to my immediate left. The artist, a chubby, pink-checked young man wearing thick glasses, began sketching with fervor, licking his lips as he did.

To my right, a painfully thin and pale young woman kept cocking her head as she observed Miki, whose expression had settled into one of supreme boredom.

I made a curved line on the paper on my easel to represent Miki's back. No. It was wrong. Too curved. I muttered under my breath as I took an eraser to it. The woman to my right was still sizing up things. I reached into the oversize black leather portfolio I'd bought for the occasion and withdrew the sketches I'd done of the male model. Now *that* was a back. I felt I'd captured the curvature of his spine rather nicely, and resumed trying to achieve the same with Miki.

Ten minutes later, Carlton asked us to stop while Miki took a break. He should have called it a breather, because she immediately slipped into her robe, opened a fire door at the rear of the white clapboard building, and stepped outside to smoke a cigarette. So young, I thought, to be hooked on a nicotine habit. If I were her mother . . . which I wasn't, of course . . . but if I were, I'd try to convince her to quit before it became too ingrained, and difficult.

Carlton strolled between easels, glancing at what we'd done during the first ten minutes. 'Good start,' he told me. The only thing on my paper was the redrawn curve of Miki's back.

'It's so difficult to get it just right,' I said.

'You did better with Willard.'

'I think you're right,' I said. 'Is it usually

easier to draw men than women?'

'Depends entirely on your sexual orientation,' he replied, a small smile on his lips.

'I didn't mean it that way,' I said.

'Of course you didn't, Mrs. Fechter.' He moved to the next easel.

As I stood waiting for Miki, the model, to return, I thought about being there on this Saturday morning. I'd signed up for the life-drawing class in the Hamptons because it was far from my home in Maine. I knew that Cabot Cove had similar classes—at least two local artists of note held them.

But I would have been too embarrassed to have taken them there. Jessica Fletcher sketching nude models? The gossip mill would have gone into high gear. My closest friends would be calling to see whether I'd slipped into senility without them having noticed it.

No. If I was to pursue this dream of mine, it would have to be done surreptitiously, at least in the early stages of my 'fling.' Perhaps one day I would be proud enough of what I'd drawn and painted to show it off to my friends. In the meantime, I was committed to remaining a closet artist. Here, in this studio in the Hamptons, I was Mrs. Fechter, who came to the class with her hair hidden under a brightly colored turban, and who was partial to oversize sunglasses that never left her nose.

Two of my 'works' hung on the walls of my

37

home. My friends visit often, but no one has ever asked who painted them. And, of course, I hadn't signed them.

'Pretty scene,' one friend said. 'Where did you get it? Flea market?'

'Nice colors. Goes with the couch.'

'Are those *birds*?'

'Are those *trees*?'

'Let's go,' Carlton said to Miki.

She snuffed out her second cigarette, came inside, and again took her position on the platform. 'We'll do fifteen this time,' Carlton said. 'Full frontal view.'

Miki faced us. A wan smile came and went. She directed a stream of air at a lock of hair that had fallen over her forehead, hunched her shoulders, allowed them to relax, and settled in for another modeling session.

Time passed quickly; I was surprised when that day's lesson was almost over. Miki had used each of her breaks to go outside to smoke. Now, she settled in for her final pose of the morning. Carlton instructed her to lean forward, with her head down between her legs, her hair skimming the floor.

'I hate this pose,' she said.

'But it's a classic,' Carlton said. 'We'll do ten minutes and call it a day.'

I'd loosened up as the morning progressed, my strokes with the pencil more free-flowing now, less constricted. My chubby colleague next to me had filled his paper with odd

38

shapes, mostly boxes and circles, his vision of Miki. I preferred mine, as imperfect as it might have been.

'Time,' Carlton announced.

I started to pack away my materials. I looked up. Miki was still in her pose. Strange, I thought. Carlton noticed it, too. He tapped her shoulder, laughing as he did. 'Hey, Miki, wake up.'

Instead of straightening, she slowly continued in the direction in which she'd been leaning. Over she went, face first.

'Good Lord!' I said, going to where she was sprawled on the cold, bare floor. I knelt and placed my fingertips on her neck. There was no pulse.

The others had formed a tight circle around us. I looked up. 'She's dead,' I said.

There were screams and muttered curses.

By the time I stood, Carlton had already called the local police. He asked for an ambulance, but I knew it was too late. I covered Miki's bare body with her robe.

Minutes later, the door opened and two uniformed officers entered, followed closely by a man and woman from the town's volunteer ambulance service.

'She's dead,' the male medic said.

'I know,' I said.

One of the officers looked at me. 'Who are you?'

'I'm . . . I'm J. D. Fletcher. I'm a student

39

here.'

'Fletcher?' Carlton said. 'I thought you were Mrs. Fechter.'

'Well, you see, I—'

The older of the two policemen narrowed his eyes. 'You that famous mystery writer?'

'I really—'

'It is,' one of my fellow students said loudly. 'It's Jessica Fletcher. I've read some of your books.'

I held up my hands and said, 'I really think who I am is beside the point. Our lovely model is dead.'

An hour later, after Miki Dorsey's body had been removed, and we'd all given statements to the police, I packed up my things, left the studio, and started walking back to the inn. I couldn't shake the vision of the lifeless young woman sprawled on the platform, her future snuffed out, her dreams and aspirations never to be fulfilled.

Dying so young violated the natural order of things. There was no rationalizing it, whether it occurred because of war or disease, famine, acts of nature, or natural disasters. The young were to live until it was time for them to die.

My eyes filled up, and I wiped a tear from my cheek. I ached for the young model named Miki. And I felt a little sorry for myself. What was to have been a pleasant foray into the world of art had ended in death, right before my eyes.

CHAPTER FIVE

The first person I saw as I approached the inn was its owner, Mr. Scott. He stood on the sidewalk as though waiting for someone. It turned out to be me.

'Are you all right, Mrs. Fletcher?' he asked.

'Yes. Well, I've been through a difficult morning, but—'

'I heard,' he said, slightly breathless. 'They're inside.'

'Who is inside?'

'Two reporters.'

'Reporters?'

'Waiting for you.'

'Oh, my.'

'They said you witnessed a murder.'

'No. Not a murder. A tragic death of a young woman.'

The front door opened and a sprightly young woman came bounding through it, followed by a young man carrying a camera. My instinct was to turn and run, but there was no time for that.

'Mrs. Fletcher,' the woman said, smiling and offering her hand. 'Jo Ann Forbes, *Dan's Papers*.'

We touched fingers.

'This is Jim Bellis, my photographer.'

'Hello,' I said. He replied by quickly raising

41

the camera and squeezing off a shot of me.

'We got here as fast as we could, Mrs. Fletcher,' Forbes said. 'As soon as we heard.'

I looked to Mr. Scott for support. All I received from him was a pained expression.

'You saw Miki Dorsey die,' Forbes said.

'Yes. It was tragic.'

The photographer kept shooting—me, Mr. Scott, the front of the inn. People now stopped to see what the commotion was. The crowd was growing.

'Maybe we'd better go inside,' I said.

'Okay,' said Forbes.

'All right, Mr. Scott?' I asked.

'I suppose so,' he replied, not sure whether he meant it.

We settled in the parlor.

'It's quite a story,' Jo Ann Forbes said.

'I don't think—it's a sad story, that's all. And I don't see why you want to talk to me. I was just another student in the class when she died.'

'Exactly,' Jo Ann said. 'The famous Jessica Fletcher, writer of best-selling murder mysteries, taking an art class and sketching naked men and women.'

'Oh, my dear, I really think that—'

'The sketch was good.'

It took me a moment to process what she'd said. 'What sketch?' I asked.

'The one you did of the naked male model.'

'Sketch *I* did? You must be mistaken.'

42

'It was delivered to the office right after we heard about the model's death. We bought it.'

'Bought the sketch I did?'

'Yes. I have tremendous admiration for you, Mrs. Fletcher, taking up art at your age.'

'Excuse me,' I said, 'but I really must get to my room. I have some phone calls to make.'

'Just a few more minutes,' Ms. Forbes said. 'Please. Give me some comments about what it was like for Jessica Fletcher to be sketching naked men.'

Mr. Scott's eyes had widened to their fullest aperture.

'Good-bye, Ms. Forbes,' I said, heading up the stairs, with Scott right behind me. Once in my room, he said, 'I'm terribly sorry about this, Mrs. Fletcher. I didn't know what to tell them when they arrived.'

'No fault of yours,' I said. 'I just need time alone to sort this out.'

'Of course. Would you like some tea?'

'That would be much appreciated.'

As he backed to the door, his eyes remained on my large black leather portfolio. I said nothing. Once he was gone, I opened the portfolio and pulled out my sketches. The one I'd done of the male model was missing. Someone had taken it in the confusion that followed Miki Dorsey's death. Who would have done such a thing? How dare someone take what was mine?

The reporter had said the sketch had been

delivered to the newspaper, and that they'd 'bought it.'

Outrageous, I thought. Someone stole my sketch in order to sell it to a newspaper, capitalizing on someone's death, and on my name. Did the paper intend to publish it? 'I'll sue,' I muttered to the empty room.

And then it struck me why I was so upset. It wasn't that someone had done this to me. It was that my precious little secret was no longer a secret. My wanting to learn to be an artist was now public knowledge.

That was the most maddening aspect of all.

Mr. Scott delivered my tea and asked if I needed anything else.

'Thank you, no,' I said. 'Are they still downstairs?'

'No, Mrs. Fletcher. They left immediately.'

'Good. Mr. Buckley hasn't called, has he?'

'No.'

'Well, maybe this all will simply go away.' I managed a smile. 'Thank you for everything, Mr. Scott.'

'My pleasure.'

He looked at my portfolio as he left.

The phone rang. It was Vaughan Buckley.

'Hello, Vaughan,' I said.

'What in the world is going on?' he asked.

'About what happened this morning? You've heard?'

'Yes. Well, I really don't know the details but—I just got a call from the editor of *Dan's*

44

Papers.'

'What *is Dan's Papers*?' I asked.

'The Hamptons' leading newspaper. Been around for, must be, thirty years. Keeps tabs on all the celebrity comings-and-goings.'

'Why did he call *you*?'

'To see if I could persuade you to give them an interview. They know me pretty well, know I publish your books. What were you doing in an art class sketching nudes?'

'I started taking up art a few years ago and— it doesn't matter. What did you tell them?'

'I said I couldn't speak for you. He mentioned something about a sketch of yours they intend to run.'

'Good Lord.'

'A sketch of a naked man?'

'Yes. Vaughan, I think it might be best if I cut short my vacation and headed back to Cabot Cove.'

'Not on your life, Jess. Did you give them permission to publish the sketch?'

'Of course not. Someone in the class stole it from my portfolio and sold it to them. I think I'll sue.'

'Was it good?'

'Was *what* good?'

'The sketch.'

'No. Vaughan, maybe we should get together. Now.'

'Sure. Olga took Sadie and Rose to be groomed. I can be there in—'

45

'Maybe we'd better meet somewhere else.'

'Yes, of course. I'd say the house, but there are workmen everywhere. The Grand Café. Ask Joe Scott to call you a cab. They all know where it is. A half hour?'

'Sure.'

The Grand Café was bustling when I arrived. Vaughan, dressed in jeans, loafers sans socks, and a white lightweight V-neck tennis sweater, was waiting for me on the sidewalk. 'I got us an outside table,' he said. 'More privacy.'

We walked through the silver and plum art deco interior to the outside dining area, which was as crowded as inside had been. Once seated, Vaughan ordered coffee and orange juice for us: 'Hungry?' he asked.

'No,' I replied abruptly.

'I am.' He ordered a frittata omelet for himself.

'I changed my mind,' I said. 'One of the muffins would be nice.'

'Blueberry?'

'That will be fine.'

'So, Jessica, tell me all about it.'

'About the young model's death? All I know is that one minute she was alive and posing for us, the next minute she was dead.'

'No idea how it happened?'

I shrugged, and offered my hands palms up. 'Heart attack? Stroke?'

'At that age?'

46

'I know. Unlikely. But what else could it be?'

Vaughan leaned closer. 'Jess, tell me about you taking up art.'

'Not much to tell. I decided that—'

'Research for your next book? Stolen art? International art theft ring? It's a hot topic these days.'

'No, Vaughan, nothing like that. I simply wanted to learn how to paint. To sketch. To create something beautiful on paper.'

'You do that with your books.'

'This is different.'

'I know. I'm not being difficult, Jess. It's just that you've kept this secret passion under wraps fur so long. Why? I think it's wonderful that you decided to pursue another creative outlet.'

'Silly, I suppose, but that's the way I wanted it to be. Until I had something worthwhile to show people.'

'I understand. Are you serious about suing *Dan*'s *Papers* if they run your sketch?'

'Probably not. I'm not the litigious type.'

'They'll play it up big.'

'Not bigger than the death of the young woman, I hope. Did you or Olga know her? Her name is—was—Miki Dorsey.'

'No.'

'I just thought you might have run across her through your connections here in the art world.'

47

'Afraid not.'

'I'd like to learn more about her.'

'I thought you wanted to go home.'

'I do. But I don't think I'll rest if I didn't have, at least, some inkling of who she was and why she died. I felt as though I knew her. She was a smoker, and I thought that if I were her mother, I'd get her to give up the habit.'

His smile was warm and genuine. He placed his hand on my arm and said, 'So typical of you, Jessica. So caring.'

'Maybe curious is more accurate.'

'Whatever. Want me to make some inquiries about her?'

'Sure. I suppose the newspaper will have some details of her life.'

'Undoubtedly. Unless she was one of thousands of young people who congregate out here in the summer, sharing group houses, taking odd jobs to pay the rent. A nude model? I suppose it pays well.'

'I certainly hope so.'

The muffin was delicious. Vaughan drove me back to Scott's Inn in his Mercedes. The reporter, Jo Ann Forbes, and her photographer, Jim Bellis, were waiting on the front porch. 'I'll handle it,' Vaughan said, walking in front of me.

'Hi, Mrs. Fletcher,' Jo Ann said to me over his shoulder.

I didn't return the greeting.

'Please leave Mrs. Fletcher alone,' Vaughan

48

said. To Bellis: 'And stop taking pictures!'

'Just a brief interview?' Ms. Forbes said.

'Maybe another time,' said Vaughan, leading me up to the porch and through the front door.

'They stole your nude sketch,' Forbes said from behind us.

I stopped and turned. 'I am well aware of that,' I said.

'No, not from you,' she said, closing the gap between us. 'From the newspaper office.'

'Who stole it?'

'I don't know, Mrs. Fletcher, but it's disappeared. The publisher, my boss, Dan, who owns the paper, blew his stack at the editor who bought the sketch. Said it belonged to you, and that he wasn't about to violate your rights by publishing it.'

I drew a breath and smiled. 'Please thank your boss for his sensitivity and ethics. You say it's now missing.'

'Yes. We had a reception this morning for a gallery owner who's opening up a branch of his Manhattan gallery in town. Fifty, sixty people milling around. I don't know where the sketch was, but it's gone. Vanished.'

'At least it won't be on your front page,' I said.

'Please, Mrs. Fletcher, won't you give me an interview about your new career as an artist?'

'I don't have a new career—as anything. I'm a writer. I paint strictly as a hobby.'

49

'Just a few minutes. Your inspirations. How you felt sketching naked models. The medium you prefer, how many pieces you've done so far, things like that.'

Vaughan stepped between us. 'Maybe another time,' he told the reporter. 'Mrs. Fletcher has had a rough morning.'

'You saw Miki die.'

'Did you know her?' I asked.

'A little. We have mutual friends.'

I looked at Vaughan, whose expression was a question mark.

'How about later?' I suggested to Ms. Forbes.

'Jessica, I think—'

'No, Vaughan, it's all right. Call me later this afternoon,' I said to her. 'Around three.'

Vaughan escorted me to my room. He closed the door and said, 'I'm not sure you should talk to her.'

'She seems nice,' I replied, looking out over the rear garden.

'You know the press, Jessica. Do you really want to go public about your art studies?'

'It's already public, Vaughan. I was very upset when I first heard that someone had stolen my sketch from my portfolio. I still am, but not nearly as much as I was. Initial shock has worn off. As long as people know anyway, I might as well relax and try to enjoy the rest of my stay.'

'That would make Olga and me happy.

We're looking forward to spending time together.'

'And we will. Thanks for breakfast, and for lending your ear.'

'Always an ear available for my favorite author. What do you plan to do for the rest of the day?'

'Hang out, as they say.'

'Oh,' he said, 'I almost forgot. We've been invited to a gallery showing at five. Thought you might like to join us before we head for dinner.'

'At five? All right.'

'Pick you up here.'

He went to the door, placed his hand on the knob, turned, and said, 'Careful what you say to the reporter this afternoon.'

'I promise. Hopefully, I'll learn more from her than she'll learn from me.'

CHAPTER SIX

It's a curse, this need of mine to get to the bottom of things.

Finding out more about the dead model, Miki Dorsey, wasn't destined to accomplish anything for me, or for anyone for that matter. As tragic as her death was, it undoubtedly resulted from some congenital defect in her physiological makeup. Like those young athletes we occasionally read about who suddenly die on the basketball court, or on the line of scrimmage. A bad draw of the cards.

But it shouldn't happen. One minute Ms. Dorsey was very much alive and posing for fifteen fledgling artists. The next minute she was dead.

I knew I could justify looking into her death based upon the theft of my sketch. Maybe I could find out who took it. Even more important, the sketch was now floating around the Hamptons. Where was it? And who had it now?

I stopped going through my internal justification process, and decided to take a walk. It was sunny and warm outside, the sort of pretty day I'd counted on when deciding to vacation in the Hamptons.

I went downstairs, passed through the empty lobby and parlor, and peeked through the curtains on the front door. No one outside, either.

Once at the sidewalk, I had a decision to make. Left or right? I took the same route I'd chosen the night before, taking me into town, past the shops and galleries. It was as I approached the gallery in which the dead young artist, Joshua Leopold, was featured that I realized I did not want to bump into the gallery owner, Maurice St. James. I left the main street a block shy of the gallery and wandered in the direction of the ocean. And toward the small white clapboard building in which the art class had been held.

Where Miki Dorsey died.

Aside from people strolling past, nothing seemed out of order when I reached it. For some reason I expected to see yellow crime-scene tape strung across the front door. But a crime hadn't taken place. Someone had died a natural death.

Of course, when any sudden and unexplained death occurs, an autopsy must be performed to rule out foul play. How long would it take to autopsy Miki Dorsey's body?

The front door was unlocked, and I entered. Everything was still; a clammy chill contrasted with the sunny warmth of the outdoors.

I went to where Miki's body had fallen. The police had used chalk to outline it. Good for them. At least they were taking prudent steps in case it turned out not to have been death from natural causes.

I eventually drifted in the direction of the door leading to the rear of the building, and the small landing where Miki Dorsey had gone for her cigarette breaks. I pushed it open and stepped outside. At my feet were her cigarette butts. I bent over and picked one up. As I did, I heard the front door open. It startled me, and I instinctively moved out of the line of sight of whomever had come into the building.

I heard the door close, and footsteps. I peered inside. A young woman stood in the middle of the room. She wore yellow shorts and a white T-shirt with an artistic design on it. Picasso?

She looked up and saw me, froze, then backed toward the front door. I stepped inside. 'Hello,' I said.

Her eyes were wide. I approached her. 'You startled me,' I said.

'Me, too,' she said. We both smiled.

'I'm Jessica Fletcher.'

'Oh, the—you're the writer who was here when Miki died.'

'That's right. Word travels fast.'

'The Hamptons thrive on gossip.'

'So I've heard. Did you know Ms. Dorsey well?'

She nodded. 'We lived together.'

'Oh. It must have been a terrible shock for you.'

'For all of us in the house.'

'How many of you live together?'

'Ten. Some are here all summer. Some just weekends.'

'I see. A group house. I've heard they're popular in the Hamptons.'

Another nod. She looked at the floor and chewed her cheek, as though deciding whether to say what she intended to say next. I waited.

'Mrs. Fletcher, did you see anything unusual just before Miki died?'

'Unusual? No, I can't say that I did. She'd been posing, and was about to stop. The

54

instructor told her the session was over. When she didn't move, he went to her. I think he thought she was kidding around. She'd said she didn't enjoy the pose she was in. He touched her, I think. Then she pitched forward.'

The girl wrapped her arms about herself and shuddered.

'I didn't get your name,' I said.

'Oh. I'm sorry. Anne Harris.'

'Nice to meet you, although I would prefer under more pleasant circumstances. Do you know what the funeral arrangements are?'

'They're doing an autopsy, I think.'

'Routine in deaths like this. Has her family been notified?'

'Her father. He's flying in from London.'

'He lives there?'

'Yes. Miki's parents have been divorced for a long time. I don't know where her mother lives. Miki never talked about her. They didn't get along.'

'Are you an artist?' I asked.

'A musician. Cello.'

'How nice. I love the sound of a cello.'

'You were taking lessons, weren't you, Mrs. Fletcher?'

'As a matter of fact, I was. I'm not very good. Just a hobby of sorts.'

'Everyone's talking about you. Chris said he met you on the jitney.'

'Chris?'

'Chris Turi.'

'Oh, yes. The nice young man who sat next to me. An artist. Does he live in your group home?'

'Weekends. He and Miki were going together.'

'A sad time for him.'

'For all of us. Are you sure Carlton Wells didn't do anything unusual to Miki before she died?'

'Carlton? Our instructor. No. Why do you ask?'

'He hated Miki.'

'I didn't sense that. Why did he hate her?'

'Because she dumped him. They used to go together.'

'I see. Miss Harris, are you telling me that you think Miki's death might not have resulted from natural causes?'

'I don't know what I think. All I know is that she was healthy before coming here for the modeling session. And now she's dead.'

I checked my watch. As I did, I realized I was still holding the cigarette butt I'd picked up outside. I dropped it into the pocket of my beige linen jacket and said, 'I must be going, but I'd like to talk to you again. Would I be imposing if I stopped in at your summer home?'

'No, that would be all right.' She gave me directions. 'It's right on the water,' she said. 'Real pretty place. But kind of grim now.'

56

'I can imagine. Well, Miss Harris, it was nice meeting you. I'll be by.'

CHAPTER SEVEN

Jo Ann Forbes, the reporter from *Dan's Papers*, called precisely at three, and we agreed to meet in a half hour at a pub in the center of town. I considered inviting her to my room at Scott's Inn, but thought better of it. Somehow, having my feeble attempts at art in the room made it off-limits to everyone but me.

The pub was pleasant, and relatively empty at three-thirty. Ms. Forbes ordered a beer called Killian Red; I settled for club soda with lime.

I took the initiative. 'What do you know about the dead model, Miki Dorsey?' I asked.

She laughed. 'I thought I was supposed to be interviewing *you*, Mrs. Fletcher.'

'We'll interview each other.'

'All right. I don't know anything about her. They're doing an autopsy as we speak. It's big news.'

'A natural death is big news in the Hamptons?'

'Sure. Young woman sharing a group home for the summer. Models in the nude to make ends meet. Famous author sketching nude models and watching her die. Former boyfriend conducting the class and known to have been dumped by dead model. Wealthy father, art dealer big-time in London, flying in. Yes, Mrs. Fletcher, it's big news, not only here but in the city, too. The *Post*, *News*, and even the *Times* have stringers out here covering it. TV, too, I hear.'

'Miss Dorsey having "dumped" Carlton Wells seems to be common knowledge.'

'Sure is. They came to blows over it.'

'Then, why did she continue to model in the nude for his classes?'

'Like I said, a need to make ends meet.'

'You say her father is wealthy. He didn't help her?'

'Evidently not.'

'What did she do for a living?'

'A little of this, a little of that. Waitressed in the city—and out here, too, on occasion. Modeled. She wasn't the classic model type—you know, tall and willowy—so she did nude modeling.'

'Do you know her current boyfriend, a Chris Turi?'

'No.' She scribbled his name in her reporter's notepad.

'Anne Harris?'

'No.' She noted that name, too.

Realizing I was giving her more information than I was receiving, I sipped my drink and fell silent.

'Mrs. Fletcher, why did you decide to take

up art?' she asked.

'I wanted to create pretty things.'

'Only reason?'

'What other reason could there be?'

She shrugged and drew on her beer. 'I hear a rumor that the sales of your books have fallen off.'

My guffaw was involuntary. 'They've never sold better.'

'I just thought—'

'That I'm looking for a new career in art? Ms. Forbes, I assure you that if that rumor were true, I do not have the artistic talent to earn a nickel.'

'I thought your sketch was pretty good.'

'You saw it?'

'Yes. Just for a minute.'

'Any word on where it might be?' I asked.

'No. But another rumor flying around town is that it's for sale.'

I hated to keep laughing at things she said; she was a lovely young woman doing a good job. But I couldn't help it. 'How much are they asking for it?' I asked.

'A thousand dollars.'

'How's the beer?'

'Delicious. My favorite.'

'I believe I'll try one.'

She was right. Killian Red had an unusual, tangy flavor. But I'm not a beer drinker, so managed only a few sips.

'Mrs. Fletcher, do you think there might

have been foul play in Miki Dorsey's death?'

'I have no idea. The autopsy will provide important information about that possibility.'

'Are you investigating it?'

'Investigating it. No, Ms. Forbes, I'm not.'

'I only ask because you're known for getting involved in real murders outside those you solve in your books. I just thought—'

'What if I were? Investigating Miki Dorsey's death.'

'Then, I'd like to be able to tag along with you.'

'I couldn't stop you. In return, will you help me find my missing sketch?'

'Sure. But why not just buy it back? You'd have it, and you'd know who took it.'

'Pay a thousand dollars for my own sketch? Absolutely not.'

She finished her beer. 'It's a deal?' she asked, extending her hand across the booth's small, scarred table.

I shook it. 'It's a deal,' I said.

CHAPTER EIGHT

Was there no end to the number of art galleries in the Hamptons?

They seemed to be everywhere, on every corner, in every nook and cranny of the area's quaint villages. It reminded me of Seattle, where bookstores dominate each intersection.

That evening, Vaughan and Olga took me to the Elaine Benson Gallery. Mrs. Benson, they told me, had been championing Hampton artists for more than thirty years, and was an active fund-raiser through her openings and shows.

The gallery was bustling with people when we arrived. Vaughan and Olga were immediately welcomed, and introduced me around. The show featured three Hampton artists, two of whom worked in acrylic, the third a sculptor whose numerous small pieces were crafted of wire and thin metal strips into pleasantly recognizable forms—horses, a carousel, trees, and buildings.

I accepted a glass of white wine from a uniformed waitress and followed Vaughan and Olga from group to group, thanking people for their kind words about my books, and hoping the facial muscles controlling my smile wouldn't give out.

I was eventually separated from Vaughan and Olga, and had to fend for myself. A woman to whom I'd been introduced earlier asked me about the rumor that I'd decided to become a visual artist. I assured her it wasn't the case. We were joined by a young couple who wanted to discuss Miki Dorsey's death, and that I'd been there to witness it.

I really didn't want to get into that subject, and tried my best to shift conversational gears.

I was succeeding, steering us into a discussion of some of the art on the nearest wall, when I spotted Maurice St. James entering the gallery.

'Excuse me,' I said, looking for the Buckleys. I spotted them in a far corner and tried to slither there through knots of people.

I would have made it were it not for the corpulent gentleman in a red bow tie who stepped in my path and insisted upon discussing the plot of a book I wrote ten years ago.

'Excuse me,' I said. 'Maybe we can discuss this later.'

His face soured. 'I just thought that you'd appreciate hearing why the plot didn't work. You see, when Cynthia came out of the schoolhouse, she couldn't possibly have—'

I rudely circumvented him and continued toward the Buckleys.

'Mrs. Fletcher!'

I was face-to-face with Maurice St. James.

'You devil,' he said, smiling and wagging his index finger in my face. 'I knew I recognized you when you were in the gallery. I checked my library at home. There you were on the cover of one of your books. Of course I knew you.'

'Mr. St. James, I really must apologize. When I said I might be interested in buying all of Mr. Leopold's work, I was joking.' I winced. 'I know, I know, it really isn't funny. It was just a whim. I—'

'My dear Mrs. Fletcher, there is no need for you to explain. I've heard of your interest in art, how you've been studying—Paris, I hear?—'

'No. No, not Paris.'

'I would be honored to represent your work, Mrs. Fletcher. We hold an esteemed position in the gallery world. We made Josh Leopold. By the way, are you still interested in buying him?' He looked left and right, then whispered, 'I can make you a'—a laugh—'an offer you can't refuse.'

Vaughan and Olga rescued me.

'You've met Maurice,' Olga said. 'Maurice, tell Jessica about the woman who came to your gallery and offered to buy everything Leopold painted.'

St. James laughed. 'I already have,' he said.

'Do you have plans this evening?' St. James asked us. 'Dinner?'

'As a matter of fact we do have plans,' Vaughan said.

'Dinner,' said Olga. 'Why don't you join us?'

St. James looked at me. 'Only if Mrs. Fletcher would not consider it an intrusion.'

'Jessica?' Olga asked.

'No, not at all.'

'Mrs. Fletcher!'

A stout woman wearing an outlandish floppy straw hat stood before me. 'Poor dear, being witness to the death of that young woman.'

Some people next to us heard, turned, and picked up on that theme.

Vaughan noticed my expression of distress, took my elbow, and led me from the crowd to the relative quiet of a distant corner. 'What's wrong?' he asked.

I let out a stream of air and shook my head. 'This is all too much for me, I'm afraid,' I said.

'Let's leave.'

'No, you and Olga stay. Enjoy dinner. I think I'm in for a quiet night alone. I didn't realize how potent this morning's experience was. It's taken everything out of me.'

'I'll get the car.'

'I can take a cab. In fact, I insist. I don't want to upset your plans. Please.'

I considered saying good-bye to Olga, Maurice St. James, and others I'd met, but the cab arrived almost immediately. 'Tell Olga I wasn't feeling well,' I said. 'And thanks for understanding.'

'Breakfast?'

'I'll call you.'

I had the driver take me directly back to Scott's Inn, where I went to my room, poured a tiny amount of brandy from a pretty decanter Mr. Scott had provided, kicked off my shoes, and pulled a chair up to the window. The gardens in back were nicely lighted, bathing the plantings in a soft, warm glow. A bright star twinkled above a large elm at the rear of the property. I couldn't see the moon, but I knew it was there, adding to the illumination from over the front of the inn.

I was sorry to have left the Benson Gallery and my friends so abruptly, but didn't feel I had a choice. My head had begun spinning, and I was afraid I might faint. Now, in the solitude of my lovely room, I felt my equilibrium returning.

I was suddenly aware of the gentle tick-tock of a wall clock, and looked at it. Six o'clock. My stomach was starting to protest. I was hungry.

I picked up the newspapers and magazines Mr. Scott had given me and thumbed through them in search of a nearby restaurant that was informal, and hopefully not busy. An ad for a small Italian restaurant caught my eye. I checked a map in the guide; it was only a few blocks from the inn.

I changed into beige slacks, a pink sweater, and new white sneakers I'd bought before coming to New York, freshened my makeup, and went downstairs, where Mr. Scott was sitting behind his small registration desk.

He looked up. 'Good evening, Mrs. Fletcher.'

'Good evening, Mr. Scott.'

'I thought you'd gone out for the evening.'

'I did, but changed my mind. I decided to spend a quiet night alone.'

He nodded. 'Anything I can do for you?'

'No, thank you. I'm going for a bite to eat. Can I bring something back for you?'

'Kind of you, Mrs. Fletcher, but no. Don't need anything.'

'Well, good night.'

The phone on the desk rang. Scott picked it up. 'Yes, matter of fact she's standing right here.' He handed me the phone. 'A Dr. Hazlitt, from Maine.'

'Hello, Seth. How nice to hear your voice.'

'And nice to hear yours, Jessica. I understand you've had quite a day.'

'How would you know that?'

'Not very difficult. Just a matter of turning on the television.'

'Television?'

'Ayuh. Had a story on the tabloid channel about you drawin' some naked models in some sort a' class, and seein' a woman model die.'

'That's basically true.'

'You *were* there, sketchin' naked models?'

'Seth, that's hardly the issue. What's important is that a young woman died.'

'Natural death, the TV says.'

'It appears that way.'

'You don't sound so certain.'

'I have no reason to believe anything else.'

'Jessica.'

'Yes, Seth?'

'I thought I knew you pretty well.'

'You certainly do.'

'You're studyin' to be an artist? I didn't

66

know that.'

'I'm not studying to be anything, Seth. Just a hobby. A new creative outlet. Stretching my horizons.'

'Ayuh.'

'I was just heading out for a bite to eat.'

'With your publisher?'

'Ah—yes, and I'm running late.'

'Aside from seein' young people droppin' dead, is everything else all right with you?'

'Of course. Everything is fine. I'm on vacation, and enjoying every minute of it.'

'That's nice to heah. Take care, Jessica. Keep in touch.'

'I will. Good night, Seth. Thanks for calling.'

I handed the phone back to Mr. Scott. 'A very good friend back in Maine,' I said.

'A doctor, huh?'

'Yes. An old-fashioned chicken-soup doctor.'

Scott laughed. 'Not many of them left.'

'Afraid not. See you later, Mr. Scott.'

The restaurant was more of a pizza parlor, with a few Formica tables justifying its 'restaurant' designation. Which wasn't off-putting to me. I hadn't had a slice of pizza in years, and it suddenly took on an almost urgent appeal.

I stepped inside the brightly lit restaurant and went to the counter, behind which were pizza pies of various types, which posed a dilemma: What kind to order?

'Yes, lady?' a young man in a tomato sauce stained white apron asked.

'A slice of pizza, please.'

'Plain?'

'With cheese.'

'Extra cheese?'

'No, not extra. Just plain. Cheese. And tomato sauce.'

He looked at me strangely, but didn't say what he was thinking, that this woman must never have had a pizza slice before. He picked up a slice from a pan and slid it into the large oven. 'Eat here, take out?' he asked.

'Eat here.'

'Drink?'

'Ah, a Coke, I suppose.'

I sat at a vacant table to wait for my pizza to heat.

Three teenage girls came in and ordered slices to eat there. They took an adjacent table. They were very loud, giggling and talking very fast. It made me smile. Was I like that as a teenager? I didn't think so, but maybe we never admit to acting in a way we find strange as adults.

The counterman was taking my slice out of the oven when the door opened. I recognized him immediately, Chris Turi, the young artist I'd met on the jitney, and who Anne Harris told me was Miki Dorsey's boyfriend.

I came up behind him as he said to the counterman, 'Three pies to go. Name is Turi.'

'Mr. Turi,' I said.

He turned, cocked his head.

'Jessica Fletcher. We met on the jitney.'

'Oh, sure, right. How are you?'

'All right. You?'

'Good.'

His one-word answer took me aback. I assumed he would have immediately mentioned Miki Dorsey's death. After all, it had happened only that morning. Anne Harris said he and Miki were going together. But here he was picking up three pizzas to go, and saying he was fine.

Was it possible he didn't know?

'Mr. Turi, I'm sorry about what happened to your—to Miki Dorsey.'

He pursed his lips and closed his eyes. When he opened them he said, 'Yeah. Incredible, huh? You were there.'

'Yes, I was.'

'Twenty-two, fifty,' the counterman said. He'd piled the three pizza boxes on the counter.

'What? Oh, right.' Turi pulled money from his jeans pocket.

As the counterman made change, I said to Turi, 'I met a young woman today at the building where Miki died. Anne Harris.'

'Anne?'

'Yes. She told me that you and Miki were—close.'

'Anne said that?'

'Yes.'

His face twisted into an unpleasant sneer.

'Perhaps she was wrong,' I said.

A smile came to his face, too quick and forced, I thought. 'It was really terrible what happened to Miki,' he said. 'So sudden and unexpected.' He was handed his change.

'Looks like you're feeding lots of people tonight,' I said.

'Your slice, lady,' said the counterman.

'Oh, yes.' I said to Turi: 'Well, again I'm sorry about Miki. Anne Harris invited me to visit the group house you share with her.'

'Did she?'

'Yes. I thought I might stop by tomorrow. Unless—'

'Unless?'

'It just occurred to me that since I'm in the mood for pizza, and since you obviously are, maybe I could have my slice back at your house.'

Was I being too forward?

'Sure,' he said. 'Good idea. Do you have a car?'

'No,' I said pleasantly. 'I don't even drive.'

'You don't drive?' His tone of incredulity was thick.

'No.'

'Great. My car's right outside. Actually, it's not mine. I don't own one. Belongs to Anne.'

Chris Turi drove too fast for my taste, but we arrived safely. The house was large, old, and ramshackle, a splendid example of waterfront elegance from another era. It was close to the shore, maybe too close in heavy weather. A wind had kicked up off the water, sending a spray into the air that was highlighted by the full moon's light. A shutter on the front of the house flapped in the breeze. Three other automobiles were parked in a circular gravel drive, dotted with clumps of weeds.

I followed Turi across the driveway and up to a porch spanning the front of the house. A board threatened to give way beneath my foot as I ascended the steps. The front door was slightly ajar. Turi pushed it open with his foot and stepped inside, carrying the three large pizza boxes. The foyer was dark. I could see that directly ahead of me was a staircase, also shrouded in shadow.

There was a shaft of light from somewhere to the rear of the house, accompanied by the sound of laughter.

'Come on,' Turi said, leading the way down a hallway to a large kitchen that opened onto an even larger common room. 'Pizza delivery,' he announced loudly to the half-dozen young people on couches and chairs. 'This is Mrs. Fletcher, the famous mystery writer.'

Anne Harris, who'd been reading a magazine, jumped to her feet and came to me. 'Mrs. Fletcher. Nice to see you again.'

'Sooner than either of us imagined,' I said.

71

'Mr. Turi and I bumped into each other at the pizza parlor. He was nice enough to invite me to—well, actually, it was me who did the inviting.'

'Hope you like pizza,' Harris said.

'I'm in the mood.' It dawned on me that I'd left my single slice back at the pizza parlor, and hadn't paid for it. I'd try to remember to stop by there tomorrow to square things.

Turi placed the pizza boxes on a large table and opened them, while Anne Harris and another young woman brought cans of beer, paper plates, and napkins from the kitchen. I placed a slice on a plate, sat in an overstuffed purple chair with some of the stuffing protruding, and balanced the plate on my knees.

'Beer, Mrs. Fletcher?' Chris Turi asked.

'No, thank you. A soft drink?'

'Diet okay?'

'Yes, thank you.'

Aside from Chris Turi and Anne Harris, the others had barely acknowledged me. A man and woman had looked up and nodded when Turi announced me, but went back to their Scrabble game, breaking only to bring their pizza and beer to where the game board was perched on an empty wooden crate. A delicate, pale young man sat on a window seat reading a book. Another woman, who appeared to be older than the others, was painting a picture in a corner. I wiped my mouth and went to her, hoping she wouldn't resent my intrusion into her creative reverie.

'That's very nice,' I said after standing silently behind her for a minute. She was painting a watercolor of a man's face, somewhat abstract but certainly recognizable for what it was.

She lowered her brush, looked at me, and smiled. 'Thank you.'

'I'm Jessica Fletcher.'

'I know. Chris brought you here?'

'Yes.'

'The grieving boyfriend.' She dabbed red paint on her brush from her palette and applied quick, delicate strokes to the painting.

'Yes, I heard he was Miki Dorsey's boyfriend. He doesn't seem especially upset over her death.'

She laughed softly and reapplied paint to her brush.

'None of my business, I suppose.' I looked around the room. The scene had all the appearance of a typical, peaceful evening at home for a bunch of college students. One of their housemates had died that morning. The feeling was eerie; I felt a chill that had nothing to do with the temperature in the house.

I was about to walk away—in fact, I decided having come here was a mistake, and wanted to call a taxi—when the artist painting the man's face said softly, 'You saw Miki die.'

'Yes.'

'Look natural to you?'

'What do you mean?'

She continued to apply brush strokes as she said, 'Did it look as though Miki had a heart attack?'

'I suppose it did. But the autopsy will determine that.'

'What did you think of Carlton Wells?'

'I thought he was a good teacher.'

'How did he treat Miki?'

'Fine. I didn't see any hostility between them.'

She sighed, turned, and looked at me with sad, knowing eyes. 'Hang around, Mrs. Fletcher. You may have the plot for your next murder mystery laid right in your lap.' With that she went to the center table and bit into a cold pizza slice.

I found Chris Turi in the kitchen. He was engaged in what appeared to me to be an angry conversation with Anne Harris. He sensed I was there and turned. 'How was the pizza?' he asked.

'Fine. Just fine. I was wondering if you'd be good enough to call me a cab. I want to get back to where I'm staying.'

'I'll drive you,' he said.

'No need,' I said.

'I insist.'

'I'll drive Mrs. Fletcher,' Anne Harris said. 'After all, it's my car.'

'I don't want to trouble anyone,' I said.

74

Ms. Harris motioned with her finger for me to follow her, and we headed down the dark hallway to the front door. We'd no sooner reached it when it opened, and a man wearing a tan trench coat, wide-brimmed brown hat, and holding a soft-sided hangup suitcase faced us.

'Can I help you?' Harris asked.

'I'm Blaine Dorsey, Miki's father.'

'Oh,' Anne and I said in unison.

'May I come in?'

'Of course. Sorry,' Anne said. We stepped aside to allow him to enter.

'I'm sorry about your daughter,' I offered.

He didn't respond to my comment, simply removed his coat and hat and tossed them on top of his luggage on the floor.

Harris and I stood mute.

'Who's in authority here?' Dorsey asked.

'In authority?' Anne said.

'Who do I talk to about Miki?'

I took the opportunity to take in Dorsey's face. He was a handsome man, in his early fifties, I judged, an Anglo-Saxon face with prominent thin nose, ruddy cheeks, heavy eyebrows, and a thin mouth. My overall reaction was that this was not a pleasant man.

'Who are you?' he asked, suddenly facing me.

'Jessica Fletcher,' I said.

'The writer?'

'Yes.'

'Why are you here?'

'I was getting a slice of pizza and—' I said to Anne, 'Could we go?'

'Sure. Miki's friends are in the back, Mr. Dorsey. That way.' She pointed to the hall.

He walked away in the direction of the light and conversation.

Anne Harris drove slower than Chris Turi had. We said nothing to each other as she navigated the streets in the direction of Scott's Inn. When she pulled up in front, she said, 'I'm glad you're here, Mrs. Fletcher.'

'Why?'

'Because there's more to Miki's death than it might seem.'

'Oh?'

'Maybe we should keep in touch, Mrs. Fletcher.'

'Maybe we should. But can you give me a hint as to why you think Miki's death was unusual?'

'Next time. I have to get back.'

'Of course. Thanks for driving me home.'

'My pleasure. How was the pizza?'

'Cold.'

'May I call you tomorrow?'

'I'll look forward to it. Good night.'

Although I'd eaten only a few bites of the pizza, I was no longer hungry. I changed into my pajamas and robe, and sat by the window that overlooked the garden. The lights were still on, and the moon's rays were as brilliant as ever.

I yawned. It was early, but I was tired. I hadn't lied to Vaughan Buckley. The events of the morning had taken something out of me. I was drained, weary—the king-size, iron-and-brass bed looked heavenly.

I cast a final glance out over the garden. At first I thought it was a cloud passing in front of the moon, casting a fast-moving shadow. But then I realized it was a person who'd been crouching behind the elm, and who now ran across the garden from right to left. The figure—male, female?—stopped for a moment and looked up at me. His, her, face was obscured by shadow. Then a final motion and the person was gone.

I thought about what I'd seen as I waited for sleep to overtake me. No reason to be concerned about it. Probably, a person taking an evening stroll and startled at seeing me at the window.

But in a private garden, behind a private inn?

Why did I wonder whether it had something to do with the unlikely death of the young nude model, Miki Dorsey?

Anne Harris says there was more to Miki's death than meets the eye.

Two people questioned the actions of the instructor, Carlton Wells, just before Miki's death.

Everyone in the group home where Miki

had lived seemed blasé about her death, with the exception of Anne Harris.

Chris Turi supposedly was her boyfriend. Yet he was the most casual of all the night of her death.

And here was I, on vacation, wanting to find out why.

'Go to sleep,' I commanded myself. 'Tomorrow is another day.'

I obeyed.

CHAPTER NINE

I awoke the following morning to the sound of rain hitting the windowpane. I looked outside. Everything was gray and wet, with a brisk wind whipping it about.

It was seven o'clock. I'd slept soundly. I slipped into my robe and called downstairs. Mr. Scott, the inn's owner, had told me breakfast was available each morning at seven, either in the small dining room, or as room service.

'Good morning, Mrs. Fletcher.'

'Good morning, Mr. Scott. Don't you ever sleep?'

He laughed. 'Not in season. Plenty of time to sleep late all winter.'

'I was wondering whether a pot of tea, some orange juice, and a dry English muffin would

78

be in order.'

'Of course. It will be up shortly, along with the newspaper. Sorry about the weather.'

'A good reading day—and to sign my books for you.'

As I waited for breakfast to arrive, I flipped through some of the local magazines and newspapers Mr. Scott had given me when I arrived, looking for an appropriate rainy-day activity.

I considered an afternoon movie, but that was too passive. There was some shopping I wanted to do before heading back to Cabot Cove—surely I could find the clock Seth Hazlitt coveted—but wasn't in the mood.

I'd settled on gallery and museum browsing when Mr. Scott delivered my breakfast. I told him of my plan for the day.

'No shortage of them around.' He sat, carefully arranging my breakfast on a small table by the window. 'I hear you've become quite the artist, Mrs. Fletcher.'

'Don't believe everything you read, Mr. Scott. In my case, don't believe *anything*.'

He laughed. 'Something else I can do for you?'

'No, thank you. This is perfect.'

Scott had brought that week's edition of *Dan's Papers*, which he'd folded over so that the front page wasn't visible to me. I took a sip of tea and opened the paper. Staring back at me was a picture of myself, one of many taken over the years to help publicize my books. The headline read: FAMED AUTHOR TAKES UP THE BRUSH—WITNESSES SUSPICIOUS DEATH OF NUDE MODEL.

I sighed and closed my eyes. It was about to start. I opened my eyes and started reading the accompanying article, bylined Jo Ann Forbes.

The sudden death of a nude model at a sketch class conducted by local artist and teacher, Carlton Wells, was shock enough. But among students in the class sketching Miki Dorsey's nakedness was none other than famed, best-selling murder mystery writer Jessica Fletcher, vacationing in the Hamptons as a guest of her publisher and his wife, Vaughan and Olga Buckley.

This reporter managed an exclusive interview with Mrs. Fletcher shortly after the tragic event. During it, Fletcher told me that rumors of falling sales of her books were false, and that she had taken up painting because 'I wanted to create pretty things.'

In a related matter, a sketch of a nude male model done by Fletcher during the ill-fated class was stolen and offered for sale to *Dan's Papers*. Dan Rattiner, owner and publisher of *Dan's Papers,* expressed outrage at the proposed sale of the sketch, which clearly belonged to Mrs. Fletcher, and declined. Then, at a party at this newspaper's offices, someone walked away with the sketch. It is currently alleged that whoever took the sketch is offering it for sale for one thousand dollars.

This reporter, at Mrs. Fletcher's invitation, is working closely with her not only to recover her sketch, but to investigate whether the sudden death of Miki Dorsey was not the result of a heart attack, or other natural cause. The results of an autopsy on Ms. Dorsey have not, as yet, been released.

I put down the paper, went to the bathroom, showered, and dressed quickly. I had the sinking feeling that this was not destined to be a day of casual browsing of galleries and museums—unless I did something to make it so.

The uneaten English muffin, untouched glass of juice, and barely tasted tea sat on the table as I put on my raincoat, stuffed a few things in my shoulder bag, and headed downstairs.

Mr. Scott was at his usual place at the small desk.

'Off on your museum tour, Mrs. Fletcher?'

'Yes.'

'How was breakfast?'

'Fine. I didn't eat much.'

'Mrs. Fletcher.'

'Yes?'

'These are for you.' He handed me a half-dozen telephone message slips.

'When did these people call?'

'Since I brought you your breakfast.'

'Oh, my.' The calls were all from media people.

'And there are some folks out on the porch looking for you.'

'The press?'

'Afraid so. I hope you don't mind my not putting these calls through. I wanted you to have a peaceful breakfast.'

'To the contrary. I appreciate the consideration. Mr. Scott, is there a back exit from the inn?'

'Yes. Two of them. And another through the basement.'

My raised eyebrows said it all.

'Follow me,' he said.

We passed through the empty dining room and kitchen to a door leading to the rear garden.

'Do you think some of them might be waiting back here?' I asked.

'Already checked, Mrs. Fletcher. The coast is clear, as they say.'

'I appreciate this.'

'I wouldn't want those damn media vultures hounding me, Mrs. Fletcher. I'll do whatever I can to help you avoid them.'

I stepped through the screen door to the garden I'd seen only from my suite's window. The rain and fog had turned everything in it a vivid verdant green. A pungent smell of flowers and manure touched my nostrils.

I walked to the elm tree and paused next to it. A vision came back of last night: the shadowy figure paused behind the tree, then running out of sight. Who might it have been? All my imagination? I didn't think so.

I was about to step away when I happened to look down to the ground next to the lovely, graceful tree. I crouched and picked up the cigarette butt that had caught my eye. It looked similar to those I'd found outside the building where Miki Dorsey had died during the class, the ones she'd smoked during the breaks. I'd forgotten that I'd put one of those butts in a jacket pocket, which was hanging in my closet. I picked up this butt, put it in my raincoat pocket, and walked with purpose through a gate to a small road running behind the Scott's Inn property. I looked up. The sky was dark and angry. The wind slapped the rain against my face, stinging it. Maybe venturing out wasn't such a good idea.

I considered returning through the garden to the house and holing up in my room until the weather cleared. But that didn't seem to be a viable option, not with the press camped on the porch.

I headed in the direction of the shore. I didn't have a destination in mind. I just wanted to get away from people, specifically the press. A boy on a bicycle passed, his head lowered into the wind. He was followed by a shaggy brown dog, who didn't look happy. A warm, dry rug in front of a roaring fireplace would be more to his liking.

I eventually reached a small street that led directly to the water, and to the town dock, according to a rustic sign attached to a telephone pole. The street was lined with small, modest homes, some in bad repair, others reflecting more active maintenance. As I walked toward the waterfront, I noticed a crudely lettered sign at the foot of a driveway: YARD SALE. At the other end of the driveway was a garage with its overhead door open. Inside, items for sale were haphazardly displayed, illuminated by a bare bulb hanging from a rafter. A man sat on a wooden chair just inside the garage.

I went up the driveway. 'Hello,' I said.

The man, who I could now see was old and gnarled, smoked a curved pipe. He nodded without getting up.

'Bad weather for a yard sale,' I said pleasantly.

'Can't do much about that,' he said.

'I suppose not. Mind if I look?'

'I'd rather you buy something.'

I laughed. 'I just might do that.'

As I perused the eclectic array of items for sale, I thought back to yard sales I'd held at my house in Cabot Cove. They were hard work, but fun. And it was always pleasing to se⌣

things I no longer wanted or needed end up in someone else's hands. I never made much money from those sales, but that hadn't been my purpose. What little cash they did generate paid for dinner out with my friends who'd helped me move items to the yard, and to tag them.

The garage contained some broken stereo equipment, frayed throw rugs, kitchen items, tools, a pile of framed pictures, worn clothing, and other things no longer of interest to the home's owner, nor to me.

I focused on the pile of framed pictures. Some looked as though they might have been painted by a small child, so crude were the images. There were a couple of prints of pastoral scenes. I held up a photograph of what I presumed was the man and his family, taken many years ago. Why did he think a photo of him and his family would be of interest to anyone else? The frame, I suppose. It was a discolored metal frame with filigree in its enlarged corners.

'You can have them all for five dollars,' he said.

'That's very—generous,' I said.

The painting at the very bottom of the pile was slightly larger than the others. I picked it up and held it away from me. It was very different from the others. It was modern in style, vivid reds and greens and yellows slashing the canvas from top left to bottom right.

'Where did you get this one?' I asked.

He turned in his chair and narrowed his eyes. 'Wife picked it up at some other yard sale. Month or so ago. Ugly, ain't it? That one you can have for nothing.'

I went to the open overhead door to catch more light on the painting. It was covered with dust, and I used the flat of my hand to clear some of it away.

'Never hung it,' said the man. 'Put it in the basement back of the water heater.'

'It is dirty,' I said. 'There's a water stain.'

'Flood. If it keeps raining, we'll have another. Like I said, take it for nothing.'

He reminded me of some old salts back in Maine. 'I will take it,' I said.

'Takin' the others?' he asked, drawing on his pipe and exhaling a stream of blue smoke.

'No thank you. Here.' I pulled a five-dollar bill from my purse and handed it to him.

'No need for that. A deal's a deal.'

'Please. I'd feel better.'

He tucked the bill into the breast pocket of his flannel shirt and said, 'Much obliged.'

'The trick now is to keep it dry,' I said.

He got up for the first time, took a shopping bag from a hook on the wall, and handed it to me. I thanked him, slipped the painting into the bag, and left.

The rain had let up some. I continued my route to the town dock and looked out over the churning waters. Many small boats at mooring bobbed in the swells; a half-dozen yachts were tethered to the dock by multiple lines. I was the only person there that morning. I took some deep breaths. As I stood there enjoying the momentary solitude, I remembered I'd promised to call Vaughan Buckley about getting together for breakfast. There was a single pay phone on the dock, and I used it. Olga answered.

'Jessica, we were getting worried about you.'

'Sorry. I made a fast exit from the inn to avoid the press camped outside.'

'I don't wonder,' she said. 'We've been getting calls all morning since the story appeared in *Dan's Papers*. Where are you?'

'At the town dock.'

'In this weather?'

'I took a walk, stopped in at a soggy yard sale. Bought a painting.'

'From a yard sale?'

'Five dollars. It's interesting.'

'We'll come get you.'

'No need. I enjoy the walk.'

Vaughan came on an extension. He asked the same questions, and received the same answers from me.

'I'll be there in a few minutes,' he said.

'If you insist.'

Good to his word, he pulled up less than five minutes after I'd hung up. 'You're soaked,' he said.

'Not on the inside.'

'What have you got there?' he asked, indicating the shopping bag.

'Oh, just a painting I bought at a yard sale.'

'Hell of a day for a yard sale.'

'More a garage sale. Where are we going?'

'Breakfast. I understand the press is hot on your heels.'

'That's what I'm told. Vaughan, any word on when Miki Dorsey's autopsy will be released?'

'As a matter of fact, there is. Heard it on the radio on the way to get you. The coroner is holding a press conference this afternoon at two.'

'Where?'

'Town hall.'

'I'd like to be there.'

'No problem. How are you feeling?'

'Fine. Sorry I ran out on you last night. I ended up at the house Miki Dorsey shared.'

'You did? How did that come about? And why?'

I recounted my quest for a slice of pizza, meeting Chris Turi, and going back to the house with him.

'How was it?' Vaughan asked as he pulled into the parking lot of the Maidstone Arms, an inn and restaurant. 'Hungry, Jess?'

'Yes. Mr. Scott brought me breakfast, but I didn't eat it. Was in too much of a rush to leave. I saw the front page of the newspaper, with my picture on it.'

'Nice shot of you,' said Vaughan, coming around to open my door. The rain was now more of a mist. We stepped into the handsome dining room, with its blue-plaid carpet, pale gold wallpaper, tables covered with crisp white linen and surrounded by ladderback chairs stained dark.

'What a pretty place,' I said as we were led to a window table.

'Olga is joining us in a few minutes. Maurice St. James, too.'

'Oh. Does he have to—join us?'

'Problem?'

I decided to tell Vaughan that I was the mystery woman who offered, in jest, to buy Mr. St. James's entire collection of Joshua Leopold's paintings. After I had, and Vaughan had stopped laughing, I added, 'Pretty foolish attempt at humor, huh?'

'I love it,' he replied. 'There's Olga and Maurice.'

They joined us, and we ordered hearty breakfasts. After coffee had been served, Vaughan said, 'Jessica told me her little secret with you, Maurice.'

'What secret?' asked Olga.

I told my story again.

'You didn't?'

'Oh, yes, she did,' St. James said. 'I'm still waiting for a check.'

'I am sorry,' I offered.

'Think nothing of it, Mrs. Fletcher. But you

might reconsider. Leopold's worth increases every day.'

'I'm sure it does. You mentioned at dinner the other night that Leopold died young, a sudden heart attack, I think you said.'

'That's right,' St. James said.

'Where did he die?' I asked.

St. James looked at Vaughan and Olga before answering, 'He died here, as a matter of fact. Why do you ask?'

'No special reason. But here we have two young, seemingly healthy people dropping dead of what's termed heart attacks. That doesn't strike anyone as strange?'

'I see your point,' Vaughan said.

'I don't,' Olga said. 'A terrible coincidence, for certain, but it's only two people. Not a dozen.'

'And a year apart,' Vaughan said.

'I suppose you're right,' I said.

'Josh Leopold was a chain smoker, too,' said Olga. 'Like Hans. Damn cigarettes. They're killers. They should be outlawed.'

'Like whiskey during Prohibition?' Vaughan said. 'That sure wasn't any answer.'

The debate on whether cigarettes should be banned was interrupted by the serving of breakfast, and the conversation shifted focus. Vaughan asked me to tell the others about the painting I'd purchased that morning at the garage sale.

'I'm not even sure I like it,' I said. 'It just

caught my eye. Too modern for my usual taste, but nice. I paid five dollars for it.'

'From how you describe it, you might have overpaid,' St. James said.

'Perhaps I did, especially when I could have had it for nothing.'

'I'd like to see it,' St. James said.

'It's in Vaughan's car.'

'When we go out,' Vaughan said.

As it turned out, everyone forgot about viewing my garage sale purchase. Maurice St. James drove away to his gallery, and Vaughan, Olga, and I got into their car. As we drove to Scott's Inn, Vaughan casually mentioned to Olga that I'd gone last night to the house in which the deceased model, Miki Dorsey, had lived.

'I wondered what you had decided to do last night,' Olga said. 'I was worried about you.'

'No need to worry,' I said. 'Miki Dorsey's father arrived from England while I was there.'

'A tragic trip,' Olga said.

'Yes. Strange, but the other young people who shared the house with Ms. Dorsey didn't seem particularly upset by her death. It was sort of business as usual there. The young man I'd met on the jitney, and who took me there, was supposedly her boyfriend, at least according to some others I've spoken to. He didn't seem too devastated, either.'

'What other tidbits did you pick up on, Jess?' Vaughan asked, a touch of sarcasm in his voice.

'Well, it seems that the instructor in our sketch class, Carlton Wells, was not especially popular. I've been asked whether he acted in an unusual way just prior to Miki Dorsey's death.'

'Sounds like the making of your next murder mystery,' Olga said.

I laughed. 'The last thing on my mind, Olga. I'm on vacation.'

'A busy one, I'd say,' Vaughan said as he pulled to the curb in front of Scott's Inn.

'I intend to correct that,' I said. I surveyed the porch. 'Looks like the press gave up.'

Vaughan turned to Olga. 'Jess wants to be on hand when the autopsy report on the model is released at two.'

Olga looked at me and smiled. 'Doesn't sound to me as though you're looking for peace and quiet. The press will be there in droves.'

'I know,' I said, sighing. 'But I'd like to hear the report firsthand.'

'I'll take you,' Vaughan said. 'How about lunch?'

'Goodness, no. I just finished breakfast. And it was very good, I might say. I think I'll catch up on some reading until two.'

'I'll be here a few minutes before,' Vaughan said.

'I'll be waiting.'

I started to get out of the car, remembered

the shopping bag with the painting in it, grabbed it, and left the car.

'A peek?' Vaughan said.

'Of this? Sure.' I removed the painting and held it up for them to see. They screwed up their faces.

I laughed. 'I know,' I said, 'it's not wonderful. But—'

'Not so fast,' Vaughan said. 'It's interesting. Reminds me of someone.'

'Just a silly impetuous purchase. Pretty slimpsy,' I said, placing the painting back in the bag.

'Slimpsy?'

'An old Maine expression. Not good quality. Well, see you later.'

Mr. Scott had left the phone messages in my room. There were now ten of them. I shoved them into my purse; I wasn't about to return any of them.

A few minutes later I strolled downstairs, entered the library, and pulled one of my books down from a shelf. I was flipping through the pages when Scott entered. 'Ah, Mrs. Fletcher, you got the messages I left for you?'

'Yes, thank you.'

'Enjoy your gallery browsing?'

'Never did get to a gallery,' I replied. 'Took a long, wet walk down to the town dock.'

'Not an especially nice morning for a walk.'

'It wasn't bad. I'm from Maine. We're used

to heavy water.'

'In a signing mood?' he asked.

'I certainly am.'

I signed each book handed me by Mr. Scott. I've always found signing books to be an especially difficult chore, especially when faced with more than one. The tendency is to want to write something clever and insightful, which is never easy off the top of your head. Still, I did my best to personalize each book to my gracious host, and eventually completed the task. He thanked me profusely, and I started to leave the room,

'Anything new about your missing sketch, Mrs. Fletcher?' he asked.

'Afraid not. I'd forgotten about it.'

'A lot of money, a thousand dollars.'

'Yes, it is.'

'Tea?'

'No, thank you.'

I lay on my bed, eyes open, and thought about the morning. I'd enjoyed my walk, even in the pouring, blowing rain. I knew I was not being especially fair to Vaughan or Olga Buckley, with my sudden disappearances and frequent unavailability.

In the meantime I gave up my pledge to spend the next few days on a quiet, carefree vacation. I wanted to know why Miki Dorsey died.

And if it wasn't from natural causes, I wanted to know who killed her.

CHAPTER TEN

'Good afternoon, ladies and gentlemen. I'm Paul Fargis, your mayor.'

Approximately fifty people were on hand for the release of the autopsy report on Miki Dorsey. Vaughan and I tried to slip into the crowd unseen, but Jo Ann Forbes, the reporter from *Dan's Papers*, spotted me and immediately approached.

'I was hoping you'd be here,' she said breathlessly.

'I wasn't sure I would be,' I said. Vaughan nodded to her.

'How do you do, sir?' she asked.

'Just fine, I read your story this morning. It was—good.'

'Thank you. I take that as a real compliment. Mrs. Fletcher, could we talk for a minute?'

'Maybe we'd better hear what they have to say up there,' Vaughan suggested, nodding toward the front steps of the town hall, where Mayor Fargis, a handsome, silver-haired man, was conferring with an older gentleman wearing a white lab coat, whom I assumed was the coroner.

'Ladies and gentlemen, could I have your attention?'

The murmur of voices faded, then ceased as

95

the mayor continued. 'As all of you know, a tragedy occurred here yesterday. A young woman—a very young woman—died suddenly. Her tender age, of course, would in itself generate interest. But her death has spurred media interest beyond that.

'When a death occurs of unknown origins, law dictates that an autopsy be conducted. This has been done in the matter of Miki Dorsey, the deceased. To present the result of that autopsy, here is Suffolk County coroner, Dr. Peter Eder.'

Dr. Eder cleared his throat, stepped to the microphone, and read from a piece of paper.

'The deceased, one Miki C. Dorsey, age twenty-four, died as the result of a coronary thrombosis resulting in a myocardial infarction. In lay terms, death resulted from a heart attack.' He stepped back to allow Mayor Fargis to retake the microphone.

'We'll take questions now,' Fargis said.

Only a few journalists asked anything. There wasn't much to ask; the official medical ruling was that Miki Dorsey had died of natural causes. Hardly newsworthy.

I looked over the crowd to where Miki Dorsey's father stood. How sad, I thought, to have to bury one of your children. He stood stoically, his face without expression, hands at his sides. Then I saw Hans Muller approach. The heavy German said something to Mr. Dorsey, who simply nodded, keeping his attention on what was going on on the town hall steps. It was obvious to me that the men knew each other, which wasn't a surprise. Both, I'd been told, were major players in the art business. And both lived in Europe.

The crowd slowly dispersed. 'Let's go,' I said to Vaughan.

But we didn't leave in time. I was spotted by reporters, and they descended upon me. Their pent-up frustration at not having anything to ask the coroner was taken out on me.

'How's your new art career going?'

'Any word on your missing sketch of the naked male model?'

'You visited Miki Dorsey's home. Are you investigating this as a possible murder?'

I tried to answer them as succinctly as possible, but each time I did, it prompted follow-up questions.

Vaughan tried to buffer me from them, gently leading me in the direction of his car. The reporters, including Jo Ann Forbes, followed, questions still coming.

'Look,' Vaughan said when we reached the car, his hands held up in a gesture that said halt. 'You're making mountains out of proverbial molehills. Mrs. Fletcher is here in the Hamptons enjoying a much-needed vacation. That she happened to be present when Ms. Dorsey died doesn't mean she thinks anything untoward occurred. She's heard the autopsy report just as you have. The case is closed. A tragic, premature natural death of a young woman. Now, please allow her to get on with her vacation.'

'But why did you visit Miki Dorsey's home?' I was asked.

'I—'

'She went to pay her respects. Ms. Dorsey's father was there, as were her friends.' He opened the door, and I got in. Vaughan came around and got behind the wheel.

As he started the car, a rear door opened and Jo Ann Forbes slid onto the seat. 'Hi,' she said. 'You promised we would work together, Mrs. Fletcher. Mind if I tag along?'

Vaughan started to protest, but I said, 'It's all right, Vaughan. I did promise Ms. Forbes that we'd—well, exchange information. I don't mind if she comes with us. She's promised to help find my missing sketch.'

Vaughan sighed. 'If you say so, Jess. Where to?'

'Scott's Inn. I have some calls to make.'

When we arrived, Vaughan said, 'Olga and I wondered if you'd like to come to the house for dinner tonight. The workmen have pretty much finished up in the dining room and kitchen, at least to the extent we can use those rooms. Lots of decorating to do, but—'

'I'd love it,' I said.

'Just a small, intimate party. A dozen or so.'

'I'm free for dinner tonight,' Jo Ann said cheerily.

Vaughan and I looked at each other.

'I'd love to do a story on the famous publisher, Vaughan Buckley and his wife, the former famous model. You're distinguished members of our summer community.'

'I really don't think that's what I want,' Vaughan said. 'We come to the Hamptons to get away from people like—'

'People like me?' Jo Ann said, her voice never losing its pleasant tune.

'I didn't mean anything derogatory,' said Vaughan.

'And I didn't take it that way.'

I smiled. So did Vaughan. 'Sure, come along,' he said. 'There's always another place at our table.'

'Terrific,' Jo Ann said. 'Formal or informal?'

Now Vaughan laughed. 'Distinctly informal, Ms. Forbes. And that means no pad and pencil.'

'On my word.'

Ms. Forbes followed me into Scott's Inn. We stopped in the entrance hall, and she peeked into adjacent common rooms. 'Wow, this is beautiful,' she said. 'I've never been here before.'

'It's very comfortable,' I said.

Mr. Scott emerged from the dining room. 'Some more calls for you, Mrs. Fletcher,' he said, handing me the message slips.

'Thank you,' I said. I introduced Jo Ann to

99

him.

'You're from the newspaper,' Scott said.

'Don't hold that against me,' she said, extending her hand. My fondness for her was growing; she had a spirit that matched her pretty young face and figure.

Scott looked at me with a quizzical expression: *Want me to get her out of here?* it said.

'Ms. Forbes will be spending some time with me, Mr. Scott. She's become a friend.'

'You should be flattered, Ms. Forbes.'

'Oh, I am, believe me,' she said.

'Come on,' I said. 'I'll show you where I hang out. It's a lovely suite.'

As we started toward the stairs, Scott said, 'Thank you again, Mrs. Fletcher, for signing all your books for me. I enjoyed what you wrote.'

Jo Ann stopped and turned to me. 'You signed all your books for him?'

'Yes. He has just about every one.'

She pulled out her reporter's notepad and started writing.

'Hardly worth noting,' I said.

'I think it is.'

The maid had been to the suite. A platter of fresh fruit and a bottle of champagne were on the small desk in the corner.

'This is beautiful,' Forbes said. She looked out the window to the English garden. 'Nice view.'

'Yes. Very nice. Now, Ms. Forbes, let's

spend a few minutes talking. Any leads on my missing sketch?'

She looked left and right, as though to see whether there might be someone listening to our conversation. 'Yes,' she said.

'I'm listening.'

'Because of the article I wrote about you and Miki Dorsey's death, I received a call this morning at the paper. A woman. She said she knew where the sketch was, and could arrange for you to get it back, through me.'

'Through you?'

'Yes.'

'Did she tell you where it was?'

'No. She's calling me again tomorrow, after I've had a chance to speak with you.'

'What's to speak about?' I asked. 'Of course I'd like it back.'

'It's still for sale,' she said.

'And I said I would not pay a thousand dollars to get back what already belongs to me.'

'Two thousand.'

'Pardon?'

'The woman said it's for sale for two thousand dollars.'

'That's outrageous! Absurd!'

Jo Ann shrugged. 'I'm just passing on what I was told by the caller.'

I said nothing.

'What should I tell her when she calls back?' Forbes asked.

'Tell her to return the sketch. No pay. No money. It rightfully belongs to me.'

'That's what I'll say.'

'Good.'

'Mrs. Fletcher?'

'Yes?'

'Your turn.'

'My turn for what?'

'Your turn to tell me something new.'

'Oh. That's right. We had a deal.'

'Exactly.'

'I'm afraid I don't have anything to share with you.'

'I don't think that's true, Mrs. Fletcher.'

'Call me Jessica.'

'You went to Miki Dorsey's home last night.'

'That's right.'

'Why?'

'You heard Vaughan Buckley. I went to—'

Her cocked head and wry smile said she wasn't about to believe what I was poised to say.

I recounted for her my bumping into Chris Turi at the pizza parlor—I still hadn't returned to pay for the slice I didn't eat—and accompanying him to the house Miki Dorsey shared with Turi and others. She took notes as I spoke. When I was finished, she looked up from her notepad and said, 'I tried to interview Miki's father this morning. He refused.'

I raised my eyebrows. 'Surely, you can't find that to be a surprise,' I said. 'I have a personal distaste for the press interviewing grieving family members, asking for their reaction to the untimely death of a loved one.'

'I agree, Jessica,' she said. 'But I wasn't going to ask that sort of dumb question. I wanted to know about a rumor that Miki Dorsey had an original Joshua Leopold painting, and that it disappeared the morning of her death.'

I'd been looking out over the garden. I slowly turned and stared at this young reporter. 'I hadn't heard that,' I said.

'Just a rumor.'

'Where did you hear it?'

'Another reporter at *Dan's Papers*. He covers the arts scene out here.'

'Strange,' I said.

'What is?'

'That she would have something as valuable as a Leopold. You told me that she had to struggle to make ends meet.'

'Her father might have given it to her.'

'But he didn't help his daughter financially. So how would she come into possession of a work by an expensive artist? Who, by the way, also died at a young age, ostensibly of a heart attack.'

'I remember when Leopold died. She might have gotten the painting before his value shot up. Happens all the time with artists. They become worth more dead than alive.'

'Some writers, too.'

'I suppose so.'

'Jo Ann, was Joshua Leopold's death as sudden as Miki's? I mean, was there the same sort of shock when it happened?'

She screwed up her face in thought. 'Yes, I suppose so, although it was very different.'

'How so?'

'There wasn't the world's most famous mystery writer present when it happened.'

I smiled. 'But it happened the same way. Alive one minute, dead the next.'

'That's right.'

'How and where did he die?'

'Let me see. He died in his studio as I recall. That's right. He was in the process of finishing a canvas when it happened. Fell into the canvas and to the floor. I remember the photograph.'

'I see. Do you know, Jo Ann, whether Miki Dorsey and Joshua Leopold knew each other?'

She shrugged.

'Would you mind if I asked you to scoot along, Jo Ann? I could use a few hours alone.'

'Sure. Thanks for having me to your room. I love it.'

'So do I.'

She looked at my large black leather portfolio. 'Your artwork, Jessica?'

'Yes.'

'Could I see?'

'Absolutely not. You run along. Give me a call about five. I'll know by then what time

104

we're going to the Buckleys.'

She left, and I glanced at the message slips Mr. Scott had given me. They could wait. I dialed the number for Seth Hazlitt, Cabot Cove's leading physician and one of my closest and dearest friends. He answered on the first ring.

'Seth, it's Jess. How are you?'

'Fair to middlin'. There's a bug goin' around that's got half the *yow-uns* laid up. You?'

'Fine. Sorry to hear so many kids are sick.'

'So's their parents. How's the vacation goin'?'

'Just fine. Seth, they just released the autopsy report on that young model who died in the figure-sketching class I was taking.'

'Ayuh. What was it?'

'The coroner says it was a heart attack.'

'Sounds right to me.'

'Seth, what else could cause death that would seem like a heart attack, but isn't?'

'Nothin' I can think of, Jessica. A fatal heart attack leaves a pretty specific set of circumstances for a coroner to see.'

'Nothing?'

'Nope. Well, there are some substances that can cause the heart to stop. A coroner who's not too meticulous might miss it, see only the result, not the cause.'

'What substances?'

'Can't tell you offhand. Sort of things you read about with spies. Exotic poisons. Nothin' for you to be thinkin' about, unless you intend to do a spy book next.'

'Not a bad idea. How can I follow up on what you've just said?'

'Call the CIA. They'll be glad to show you around; maybe even demonstrate how they can kill somebody and make it look like a heart attack.'

'You're being facetious, Seth.'

'Ayuh, that I am. Anything else I can do for you, Jessica? I got a waitin' room full a' yow-uns out there wantin' Doc Hazlitt to give 'em the magic pill that'll make 'em better.'

'Then you get to them, Seth. Thanks. I'll call again.'

'Make sure you do that.'

I no sooner hung up when I heard a cough just outside my door. I quickly opened it. Jo Ann Forbes was just about to head down the stairs. She smiled weakly. 'I was just— admiring these paintings on the hall wall.'

'Oh. They are pretty.'

'I'll call later, Jessica.' With that, she went down the stairs two at a time.

I closed my door, stood in the middle of the room, and pursed my lips. It seemed I'd better be on my toes where the charming Ms. Jo Ann Forbes was concerned. She may be pleasant, but she was also a reporter, and an ambitious one at that.

Admiring the paintings in the hall, indeed.

CHAPTER ELEVEN

I checked my watch. Three o'clock. That made it nine in the evening in Europe.

I pulled out a small address book I always carry with me, found George Sutherland's home number in London, and dialed it.

George Sutherland is a senior inspector with Scotland Yard. I met him years ago when I was in London to address a mystery writers' convention. While there, I stayed with a friend, Marjorie Ainsworth, then the grande dame of murder mystery writers. While a guest in her mansion in the tiny town of Crumpsworth, someone drove a knife into her as she slept, and I found myself not only giving a speech, but helping solve her murder. That's how I met George. He was called into the case, and we became friendly.

Just so there isn't any misunderstanding—there has been with my two best Cabot Cove friends: Dr. Seth Hazlitt and our sheriff, Morton Metzger—George and I have never been romantically involved. I'll be honest. I find him to be the most handsome and charming man I've met since the death of my husband many years ago. And yes, my thoughts sometimes stray to romance. But that's as far as it's ever gone. We keep in touch by letter and the occasional phone call, and ended up together for a week in San Francisco, where I was promoting one of my books, and he was attending an FBI conference on forensic investigation techniques. That week turned into a repeat of my London adventure—I helped solve a murder, which freed a woman falsely convicted of the crime. I even wrote a book based upon the experience, *Martinis & Mayhem.*

'George?'

'Jessica. What a pleasant surprise.' I always smile when I hear George Sutherland's voice. He's Scottish by birth, born in Wick, Scotland, on the northernmost coast. His brogue delights me. 'Where are you?' he asked. 'London, I hope.'

'Afraid not, George. The Hamptons. On the eastern end of Long Island.'

'On a holiday? Or working as usual?'

'It started as a holiday.'

He laughed. 'Don't tell me. Someone has been murdered, and Jessica Fletcher is hot on the trail.'

'Something like that,' I said, joining his laughter. 'George, I thought you might have some knowledge that would be helpful to me.'

'I hope you're right, Jessica. What do you need?'

'I need to know about poisons that can kill a person, but make it look like a heart attack, even to a trained coroner.'

There was silence on the other end.

'George?'

'Yes, I'm here, Jessica. Why do you want to know this?'

'George, I'm not intending to use such a substance, if that's what you're thinking.'

'Never entered my mind.'

'I would hope not.'

I explained the circumstances of Miki Dorsey's death, and mentioned that Joshua Leopold had died the same way.

'And you think their deaths might not have been natural.'

'I don't know what to think. But I am curious.' I told him what Seth Hazlitt had told me.

'And how is your Dr. Hazlitt?'

'Just fine. Busy, as usual. Do you know of any such substances, George?'

'Not offhand, but there are those I can ask. Which I will do first thing in the morning.'

'I appreciate it.'

'I always enjoy doing you a favor, Jess, because then you owe me one.'

'Just ask.'

'Come visit me here in London. Better yet, spend that week with me in Wick we've talked about for too long.'

'I still intend to do that, George. Maybe later this year.'

'Set a stoot hert to a stey brae.'

'What?'

'The   harder   the   task,   the   more determination is needed. An old Scottish expression. My father, rest his soul, was fond of it. More determination is needed to get Jessica Fletcher to visit me in my Wick homestead. A castle, actually. Lovely views.'

'So you've said. Call you tomorrow night?'

'Unless I call you first. Where are you staying in the Hamptons?'

I gave him the Scott's Inn phone number. 'Oh, one other thing, George.'

'Yes?'

'Could you—would you also check on a gentleman living in London? His name is Blaine Dorsey.'

'American?'

'Yes.'

'What's he do for a living?'

'He's involved in the art world in some capacity.'

'Oh, *that* Dorsey.'

'You know him?'

'Know of him. A bit of a rogue, Mr. Blaine Dorsey is. Lots of speculation about him and the way he does business. He's been under investigation for quite a while.'

'Really? What's he suspected of?'

'Art theft. No, I take that back. More of a fence for stolen art. A middleman.'

'I see. He's never been arrested?'

'Not as far as I know, but I can check on that, too.'

'Thanks, George.'

110

'We'll talk,' he said. 'Pleasant dreams.'

'It's only the afternoon here.'

'Of course. Well, wish *me* pleasant dreams. It's been a long, hard day.'

'Pleasant dreams, George. *Guideen nicht.*'

A loud laugh. 'Nicely done, Jessica. I'll make a Scot of you yet. And good night to you, too.'

CHAPTER TWELVE

My next call was to Anne Harris. I'd promised to get in touch again, although I wasn't calling because of that promise. I wanted to talk with her, hopefully to shed some light on what I'd just learned from Jo Ann Forbes, that Miki Dorsey owned an original Joshua Leopold painting, and that it disappeared the day of her death. I also wanted to learn what I could about Miki's relationship with her art-dealing father—or, if George Sutherland was correct, her *shady* art-dealing father.

The phone at the house Miki shared with friends was answered by a woman, who said Anne wasn't there.

'Would you tell her Jessica Fletcher called?' I said.

'Hello, Mrs. Fletcher. This is Waldine Peckham. I was painting when you were here last night.'

111

'I remember.'

I also remembered what this woman, whose name I now knew, had said about Miki Dorsey's death. Actually, it wasn't what she'd said as much as how she'd said it: her voice dripping with sarcasm when she mentioned Chris Turi's flat response to his girlfriend's death, and her snide comment about Carlton Wells, our art instructor.

'Enjoying your stay in the Hamptons?' she asked.

'Very much. It's lovely here. Reminds me a little of where I live, Cabot Cove. That's in Maine.'

'I know.'

'Ms. Peckham, you said a few things last night that trouble me.'

'Did I?'

'You were critical of Chris Turi's way of reacting to Miki's death.'

'Didn't you find it strange? She dies, and he goes out for pizza.'

'You're the second person who asked me about Carlton Wells.'

'A swine.'

'That's certainly direct.'

'Just telling it like it is, Mrs. Fletcher.'

'When do you expect Anne to return?'

'I have no idea.'

'Has Mr. Dorsey been spending much time there?'

'Just last night. He stayed maybe a half

hour. Didn't have anything to say, just went into Miki's room and closed the door.'

'And when he came out?'

'Looked more mad than sad to me, Mrs. Fletcher. Put on his hat and coat and stormed out of the house.'

'Well, Ms. Peckham, it was nice meeting you. How's the painting coming?'

'I trashed it. I trash everything I paint.'

I didn't know how to respond, so I simply said good-bye and hung up. Ms. Waldine Peckham was obviously not a happy woman.

I turned on the small TV in the suite and dipped through the channels. Nothing interested me, so I turned it off and tried to get back into the book I'd started on the jitney from Manhattan. I couldn't focus on that, either.

Then it dawned on me that I still owed for my slice of uneaten pizza. A good excuse for a walk. I put on a light windbreaker, went downstairs and to the street, turned right, and took the route I'd taken last night. The same young man was behind the counter when I entered. I told him why I was there, and placed money on the counter.

'No need,' he said. 'Hey, you're the lady in the paper.' He pointed to a copy of *Dan's Papers* lying on the counter, my face looking up at me.

'Oh, that,' I said. 'My fifteen minutes of fame.'

'Huh?'

'Just take the money. Your pizza is very good.'

'You left with that guy.'

'That's right. I "left" with that guy.'

'You know what I think?'

'About what?'

'About what happened to that model who died?'

'Tell me,' I said.

'I think she didn't have no heart attack. I think somebody killed her.'

'Any proof of that?'

He shrugged. The phone rang. 'Pizza Heaven,' he said into the receiver. I took the opportunity to leave.

I headed in the direction of Scott's Inn, but found myself detouring toward the gallery I'd stopped in the first night, the one owned by Maurice St. James. It was empty when I arrived, and I stepped inside, causing a tiny bell to sound that I hadn't heard the first night I was there. I waited for someone to emerge from the back. No one did.

Just as well, I thought. I was interested in looking more closely at Joshua Leopold's artwork without having to make conversation.

I went to the first painting, assumed what I felt was a proper distance to provide perspective, and looked intently at it. As I did, it took shape in the midst of its violent swirls of seemingly random color and slashes of crude black lines. I wasn't sure what shapes I saw, but there was more than chaos in the work.

I moved to the second painting, a larger vertical one that was more subdued.

As I continued around the room, my appreciation for Joshua Leopold was enhanced. It was almost as though I now understood what he was trying to convey, although I knew those with greater insight would probably consider my reactions sophomoric, at best.

I'd traveled one wall of the large space, and was about to turn the corner to take in the back wall when I heard voices. I paused and held my breath. The voices were male, and came from somewhere behind the wall.

'. . . And I will not tolerate your arrogance. I simply will not put up with it.'

'Shut up, Maurice. This is business. Why the hell do you think Hans and I have gone to the extent we have to . . . ?'

I'd moved slightly to my right to get closer to the voices. In doing so, I bumped into a small table on which a piece of sculpture was displayed. Fortunately, it was metal. It fell off the stand to the floor, making a racket but suffering no damage. My ego was another matter.

A door opened, and Maurice St. James stepped through it. 'Mrs. Fletcher,' he said, eyes wide, voice slightly higher than I remembered it to be.

'Mr. St. James.'

'What a pleasant surprise.' He quickly regained his usual composure.

'I was just admiring Mr. Leopold's work.'

'Wonderful. Still interested in buying the lot?'

'Afraid not.'

I looked past him to the door through which he'd arrived. I only saw him for a moment, a fleeting glance, but enough to know who it was. Miki Dorsey's father.

'I hope I'm not interrupting anything,' I said.

'Of course not. I didn't hear the bell. It isn't very loud.'

Not as loud as your voices, I thought.

'May I act as your guide?' St. James asked, glancing over his shoulder, seeing that the door was open, and closing it with his foot.

'No need,' I said. 'Actually, I was enjoying a solitary tour of the art. Very relaxing, very soothing.'

He forced a laugh. 'Few refer to Josh Leopold as "soothing." But it is, after all, in the eye of the beholder.'

'As it should be. Please, don't let me take you from your—meeting.'

'Meeting? I—'

I moved away from him and began looking at the other paintings on the wall. I glanced back. His smile was pasted on his face, but

116

there was a worried look in his eyes. I smiled. He did a little bow from the waist, then opened the door and disappeared through it.

I'd lost interest in viewing any more of the art on the walls.

What was Miki Dorsey's father doing there discussing what sounded like serious business? His daughter was dead only two days. What kind of a man was he?

Maurice St. James reemerged. 'Any questions about the work?' he asked.

'Yes,' I said. 'I understand that art theft is common. Have any of Mr. Leopold's works disappeared?'

It was a thin smile.

I waited for a reply.

'Disappeared? I don't think so.'

'Is he a—what would you call it?—was Mr. Leopold a hot item in other parts of the world?'

'Yes. His reputation has begun to develop a strong foreign following.'

'Was he a prolific artist?'

'Extremely. Remarkably so.'

'So this gallery represents only a small percentage of his work.'

He drew a deep breath; he was obviously annoyed at my questions.

'I don't mean to ask so many questions, Mr. St. James, but I might be interested in buying some of his paintings. I think knowing how many pieces of his art exist would have

117

something to do with the value of each piece.'

'Very astute, Mrs. Fletcher. And you're right. It does have a bearing. To answer your question, yes, what you see on these walls is only a small portion of his overall artistic output.'

'That would diminish his worth. Supply and demand, I believe it's called.'

'That's right. I think you might—'

The door opened, and Dorsey poked his head into the gallery. 'Maurice!'

'Mr. Dorsey,' I said, stepping in his direction and extending my hand. 'Jessica Fletcher. I met you last night at the house where your daughter lived. I'm terribly sorry about what happened.'

He had no choice but to take my hand, although his sour expression said loud and clear he wasn't happy to see someone else there.

Dorsey dropped my hand and said to St. James, 'Maurice, please.'

'Excuse me, Mrs. Fletcher,' St. James said. 'Please continue to browse. I'll be—back there—in case you have any questions.' With that, he disappeared with Dorsey behind the wall.

I left immediately, returned to the inn, and ordered up tea. After Mr. Scott had delivered it, I sat by the window and thought about everything that had happened since my arrival in the Hamptons.

Nothing tangible had occurred to cause me

to question how Miki Dorsey had died. A heart attack, according to the coroner.

But another young person, part of the Hamptons' art scene, had also died of a 'heart attack'. Joshua Leopold.

Miki Dorsey supposedly had an original Leopold that disappeared from her room right after she died.

Her father flies in from London and immediately starts conducting business with Maurice St. James, whose gallery features Joshua Leopold. And Dorsey obviously knows the German art collector, Hans Muller.

Miki Dorsey's alleged boyfriend, Chris Turi, doesn't act like a grieving boyfriend.

Everyone views the art instructor, Carlton Wells, as a swine, as Waldine Peckham put it.

My sketch of a male nude model is stolen and offered for sale, the price now up to two thousand dollars.

I saw a shadowy figure in the garden behind my suite.

And—

The phone rang. It was Vaughan Buckley, saying he'd pick up me and the reporter, Jo Ann Forbes, at six.

'I'll let her know,' I said.

'How did you spend the rest of your day?' he asked.

'Relaxing.'

'Exactly what I want to hear, Jess. We'll make sure the evening is a relaxing one, too.'

CHAPTER THIRTEEN

It was no surprise to me that despite the renovations being done to their Hamptons weekend home, the dinner party Vaughan and Olga held was lavish.

Jo Ann Forbes and I were two of a dozen guests. I wondered how Jo Ann would handle herself in what basically was a sophisticated, well-heeled crowd. I needn't have been concerned; she was poised and at ease with the flow of conversation that ran the gamut from politics to publishing, art to travel, fashion to food.

The only person I knew, aside from the host and hostess, was the German art collector, Hans Muller. He seemed even bigger than when I'd met him at dinner at Della Femina. His suit was rumpled and stained, as was his shirt, its collar too tight for his sizable neck. His ruddy skin had a constant sheen from perspiration. And, of course, he was never without a cigarette between his fingers. Vaughan and Olga, good sports that they are, made sure there were ashtrays on every table.

Ms. Forbes and I stayed pretty much together until a couple, introduced as publishing colleagues of Vaughan, got into a serious conversation with her about the state of media coverage of celebrities. I drifted away from them and found myself face-to-face with

120

Hans Muller, who'd gravitated to a corner of the sprawling living room.

'Ah, Mrs. Fletcher,' he said, taking my hand with the one not holding a cigarette. 'What a pleasure to see you again.'

'Likewise, Mr. Muller. What a lovely home.'

'To be expected of people of taste. Cigarette?'

'I don't smoke.'

'You and everyone else here. As usual, Hans is the only one.'

'Does that bother you?'

He laughed. 'To the contrary. It gives me a certain exclusivity I enjoy. What did you think of the autopsy report this afternoon on poor Ms. Dorsey?'

'Tragic. So young.'

'*Ya*. Fate can be cruel. So tell me, Mrs. Fletcher, are you enjoying your stay?'

'Very much.'

'And are your skills as an artist improving?'

'Probably not. I haven't tried my hand since the morning Ms. Dorsey died.'

'Pity. I understand one of your sketches is commanding a pretty sum on the open market.'

I laughed. 'Oh, that? So I hear.'

Muller looked past me. Seeing that no one was within hearing distance, he leaned closer and said, 'Mrs. Fletcher, it might be beneficial to both of us if we got to know each other a little better.'

'Oh? Why is that, Mr. Muller?'

'I believe we could strike a mutually

121

advantageous business relationship.'

'A business relationship? What sort of business?'

He smiled, exposing his yellowed teeth. 'Would you be my guest at dinner tomorrow night, *bitte*?'

'I don't know. I have other commitments during my short stay in the Hamptons.'

'I am sure you do.' He lit a cigarette. 'But, I assure you, the restaurant will be excellent, the wine rich and full-bodied, and the conversation stimulating.'

'And smoky,' I said.

'And smoky. Will you? Dine with me tomorrow?'

'Yes.'

'Splendid.' He exhibited his widest smile of the night. 'But let's keep it between us, shall we? There's so much gossip here, so many snooping people. You brought one with you this evening.'

'Miss Forbes? She's promised to simply enjoy the party. No notes. No tape recorder.'

'You're very trusting, Mrs. Fletcher.'

'At times. Well, I think I'd better talk with others. Will you call me? I'm at Scott's Inn.'

'First thing in the morning. Enjoy yourself. It's a charming group the Buckleys have gathered together this evening.'

I no sooner walked away from Hans Muller when serious doubts about having dinner with him surfaced. I rationalized as the evening wore on that there was nothing to lose by joining him at a restaurant. Besides, it might provide the opportunity to learn more about Miki Dorsey's father, who obviously knew the corpulent German.

Olga—more accurately, two members of her house staff under her direction—put out a lovely meal: A red pepper soup with garlic croutons, a salad of mozzarella, tomatoes, and onions drizzled with a lovely light dressing, grilled pepper-crusted salmon steaks with cucumber relish, asparagus roasted in olive oil, and for dessert, fresh peach pie. The white wine served with dinner was exquisite, at least to this palate. Vaughan said it was a 1993 Riesling *Grafenreben* that he personally favored. No argument from me.

I occasionally glanced over at Jo Ann Forbes, who seemed to be having a wonderful time. As had happened at the restaurant, Hans Muller was becoming drunk and sleepy, something I'd better keep in mind when we had dinner.

We left the dining room after dessert to enjoy coffee and brandy in what Vaughan described as the library. Like every other room in the house, it was oversize. One long wall was dominated by floor-to-ceiling bookcases. Other walls held a variety of paintings hung close together.

'This is the one room we're not renovating,' Vaughan said after toasting our being together. 'And you can see why we're redoing the place. Walls should never be this cluttered.'

'And lots more to hang, I understand,' said a guest.

Olga's face lit up. 'We have been on a buying spree,' she said. 'I'd forgotten how much fun art auctions can be. We've picked up some marvelous pieces.'

'An unveiling?' Hans Muller asked.

'Now?' said Vaughan. 'They're all standing on the floor of a spare room.'

'So what?' said another guest. 'Come on, Vaughan. Show off your purchases. No false modesty.'

The spare room was empty, except for dozens of framed paintings leaning against each other in a corner.

'Will you do the honors?' Vaughan asked Olga.

'Sure.'

She slowly displayed each work, angling it so that it caught the light from overhead track lighting. Vaughan narrated:

'We decided not to limit ourselves to any style or period. And, more important, we did not buy anything with an eye toward making a profit. We invested in what our eyes responded to, not any quest for appreciation.'

As they went through the works, some of the names struck me as being artists of great reputation and value. There was a small impressionistic sketch by James Ensor, an original Kandinsky, a self-portrait by Oskar Kokoschka, and an original Stella montage. I was impressed. Although the names were only vaguely familiar to me, I knew they'd cost the Buckleys a great deal of money.

'We bid on an early Monet,' Vaughan said, 'but we lost out to an anonymous bidder from Europe.'

'A shame,' said a guest. 'No home is complete without an original Monet.' His comment brought forth laughter.

Olga continued to show the artwork in the room while her husband commented on each piece. It was when she pulled out the next to last piece to be shown that Hans Muller, who'd almost dozed off leaning against the wall, came to life. 'Wait,' he said.

'Like this one, Hans?' Olga asked.

'Who is it?' Muller asked, his words slightly slurred.

'The one unattributed piece in the bunch,' Vaughan replied. 'No artist's signature. We're planning to have it appraised, hopefully to discover it's by Pollock. It could be, wouldn't you agree?'

The painting was distinctly modern. Colors were splashed across the canvas in what seemed to be random patterns, vivid colors, reds and purples and yellows and orange.

Muller stepped to where Olga held the painting, and leaned forward to better see it.

'Your opinion?' Olga asked the big German.

'Powerful,' he said. 'A bold statement.'

'Like your current favorite artist, Josh

Leopold,' said Vaughan.

'It is not a Leopold,' Muller said. 'Yet— where did you get this?'

'An estate auction last weekend,' Olga replied.

'Here? In the Hamptons?'

'As a matter of fact, yes. Just a few miles from here.'

Muller frowned. He turned to Vaughan and said, 'I would like a few days with this painting.'

'Oh?'

'To examine it. It has—well, you know it is of a style and school in which I have a special interest. Just a few days at my leisure. *Ya?*'

Olga and Vaughan looked at each other, then said in unison, '*Ya.*'

The party broke up shortly after that. Vaughan offered to drive me and Jo Ann Forbes home, but another couple, he an investment banker, she a fashion designer, insisted they were passing Scott's Inn anyway and would be pleased to provide transportation. Vaughan called a cab for Hans Muller, who left cradling the painting in his arms.

'It was wonderful having you,' Olga said to me. 'And you, too, Ms. Forbes.'

'It was gracious of you allowing me to invite myself,' Jo Ann said. 'I had a wonderful time. And I kept my promise. No notebooks, no tape recorders.'

Olga laughed. 'It wouldn't have mattered. Nothing newsworthy here tonight, just good friends enjoying themselves.'

'And a mini-education in art,' Forbes said. 'Again, Mrs. Buckley, thank you. It was a great evening.'

The couple who drove us back offered to take Jo Ann to where she lived, but she insisted upon getting out of the car with me. When they drove off, she asked, 'A nightcap, Mrs. Fletcher?'

'Afraid not. This lady is ready for bed.'

'I understand. Did you find Mr. Muller's behavior strange after he saw that painting, the one he took with him?'

'No. You did?'

'I guess not. It's just that ever since Miki Dorsey died, I find myself suspicious of anyone with an interest in art.'

'I suggest you get over that,' I said pleasantly. 'If you don't, you include the Buckleys and me in that perception.'

'I didn't mean anything by it,' she said defensively.

'Of course you didn't. And to be honest, I share a little of that—may I call it paranoia?'

She giggled. 'Call it anything you want. Can I call you tomorrow?'

'Sure. How far do you live from here?'

'Not far. By the water. A short walk. Not far from Mr. Muller's beachfront cottage. Good night, Mrs. Fletcher. Jessica.'

'Good night, Jo Ann. I'll look forward to hearing from you.'

127

It wasn't until I was in my suite that I wondered why she knew where Hans Muller lived. Probably because she's a reporter, curious about everyone and everything, I decided.

But she was right. Muller's intense interest in that particular painting did seem unusual. Then again, everyone involved in the world of art seemed—well, a little strange. Including Hans Muller.

CHAPTER FOURTEEN

The ringing phone jarred me awake. I fumbled for the small travel alarm I'd placed on the table next to the bed, and held it up to catch moonlight pouring through the windows. Four o'clock.

In the morning!

It kept ringing. I picked up the receiver and mumbled, 'Hello?'

'Mrs. Fletcher.'

The German accent came through loud and clear.

'Mr. Muller?'

'*Ya*. I woke you.'

I almost laughed. 'Of course you woke me. It's four in the morning.'

'*Ya*. I am sorry, Mrs. Fletcher. But a terrible thing has happened. I didn't know who else to call. Your number was the first that came to me.'

My bad luck, I wanted to say. Instead, I said, 'What has happened that is so terrible?'

'Your Ms. Forbes.'

'*My* Ms. Forbes?'

'The reporter.'

'I know who you're talking about, Mr. Muller. What about her?'

'She—is—dead!'

I snapped on the bedside lamp and sat up straight. I heard Muller breathing heavily on the other end of the line. Was he crying?

'Mr. Muller, please get a hold of yourself. You say Ms. Forbes is dead? How do you know that?'

'Because she is here.'

'There? With you?'

'*Ya*. At my house.'

'How? Why? What happened?'

'I don't know. I arrived here a few minutes ago and found her. In my bedroom. Dead! *She is dead*!'

'My God,' I muttered to no one in particular. It then occurred to me that it was four A.M. Muller left the Buckleys when I did, at about eleven-thirty. Why was he just now arriving home? I asked.

'Please, Mrs. Fletcher. I will explain everything when you come.'

'You expect me to come now? Have you called the police?'

'No. I don't know what to do. I am a stranger here. You have dealt with such things before. Please. *Bitte.* Come now.'

I sat on the edge of the bed and shook my head to dislodge the last remaining cobwebs of sleep. 'All right. Where do you live?'

He gave me the address.

'I'll be there as soon as I can. In the meantime, do not—I repeat—do not touch anything. Do you understand?'

'*Ya.* I will touch nothing.'

I threw on some clothes and started downstairs on tiptoe. I didn't want to wake any other guests. I remembered that a list of taxi service numbers was posted on the wall next to Mr. Scott's desk.

But as I descended the stairs, I realized that someone had to have put through the call to my room. There was no direct dial at Scott's Inn. I was right. Mr. Scott, wearing a bathrobe and slippers, was at the desk.

'I'm so sorry, Mr. Scott,' I said.

'He said it was an emergency. Otherwise, I wouldn't have put the call through.'

'I understand.'

'Is everything all right?'

'No. Well, it probably is, probably just a mistake. But I have to respond. Are any taxis working this hour?'

'Two run all-night service. Want me to call one?'

'Please.'

A minute later, a cab pulled up in front of the inn. 'Again, Mr. Scott, I'm sorry you had to be awakened at this ungodly hour.'

He smiled; bless him. 'Goes with the business, Mrs. Fletcher. You never know what's going to happen when you run an inn.'

The driver was a pleasant older man who immediately asked why I was heading for the beach at this hour.

'A friend is sick,' I replied.

'Sorry to hear that. Need a doctor?'

'I don't think so, but thanks for suggesting it.'

I'd forgotten how close Scott's Inn was to the shore. We arrived at the narrow street leading down to the water in five minutes. Muller's cottage was at the end of the street, the one closest to the coast. A yellow light glowed on a small porch, and lights inside could be seen through the windows. I strained to see a sign of Muller through the fog, but saw nothing. The only thing of which I was aware was the sound of waves hitting against the shore.

'Maybe I should wait until you check on your friend,' the driver said.

'No, that's not necessary. On the other hand—'

'Go on in, ma'am. I'll be here until you give me the okay sign.'

'Fine. Let me pay you.' I handed him the fare, opened the door, and approached the cottage, stopping once to look back at the driver. He waved. I returned the wave. A nice man.

I slowly ascended the three steps to the porch and went to a window. Through it I could see a source of illumination, a table lamp that cast a weak pool of light over what appeared to be a living room. I stepped closer and tried to take in the entire room. I saw no one.

I knocked on a screen door. When there was no response, I tried again, harder this time. I heard footsteps, heavy ones, and then the inner door opened.

'Here I am, Mr. Muller.'

'*Ya. Ya. Danke.* Thank you for coming, Mrs. Fletcher.'

I looked back to where my cabdriver waited. He'd turned on the vehicle's interior light; I could see him straining to see what was happening at the cottage door.

'Come in, come in, *bitte.*'

'Where is Ms. Forbes?' I asked.

'In the bedroom, as I told you.' He looked past me to the taxi. 'Who is that?'

'A cabdriver. He drove me here.'

'Tell him to go away.'

'Why?'

'Please.' Muller pushed past me and went to the edge of the porch. 'Go away!' he shouted at the driver.

I came up behind him and touched his broad back. He wore the same white shirt he'd worn at the dinner party. It was wet with his perspiration. 'Mr. Muller, take me to Ms.

Forbes,' I said coldly and flatly.

The cabdriver started to get out of his car, but I said, 'Everything is all right. You can go. Thank you for staying.'

'You sure, lady?'

'Yes, I'm sure.'

Muller and I watched the driver make a U-turn and drive away. Muller turned to me. 'Come on,' I said. 'I didn't come here at four in the morning to admire the ocean.'

I followed Muller inside, where we stood in the center of the cramped living room. He took a deep breath, squeezed his eyes shut, opened them, and pointed to an open door.

I went to the door, which led to the cottage's only bedroom. It was dark. I ran my hand over the wall just inside in search of a light switch. There wasn't one. I turned to Muller. 'Where's the light in here?'

I stepped aside to allow him to enter the room. He went to the bed, reached above the headboard, and turned on a twin wall light with tulip-shaped clear-glass shades. I took in the room.

'Where is she?' I asked.

'There. Behind the bed.'

I tentatively skirted the unmade double bed and peered over it. There, between the bed and the wall, was Jo Ann Forbes. She was on her back. Her eyes were wide open. So was her pretty mouth. One hand was on her chest, the other on the floor at her side.

I leaned closer. The lamp provided minimal light, but enough to allow me to see that there was blood on one side of her face, her left cheek, and up into her hairline.

I stepped back and sighed. Muller stood in the doorway. I turned to him. 'You found her exactly the way she is?' I asked.

'*Ya*. Just like she is.'

'You didn't touch her?'

'No. No, not true. I picked up her hand to see if there was a pulse.'

'You did?'

'Yes. The hand on her chest. I put it there.'

'What else did you touch, Mr. Muller?'

'Nothing.'

'She had nothing in her hands?'

He paused, too long for comfort.

'Mr. Muller?'

'No. Nothing. In her hands.'

I went to the living room. 'Where's the phone?' I asked.

'In the kitchen.'

The kitchen was a Pullman type, very small and with a mini-refrigerator, two-burner stove, and a microwave unit. It struck me as I entered it that the cottage was remarkably Spartan for a man I assumed was a wealthy art dealer and collector. I would have expected him to rent more lavish quarters while in the Hamptons.

The white wall phone was over the short, narrow countertop. I picked up the receiver and dialed 911. A woman answered on the first

134

ring. No surprise. How many 911 calls would be made at this hour in a resort area like the Hamptons?

'My name is Jessica Fletcher. I'm calling to report a death.'

'Jessica Fletcher. The mystery writer?'

'That's right.'

'Where are you?' the 911 operator asked.

I gave her Muller's address.

'Please stay right there, Mrs. Fletcher. I've dispatched someone.'

'I will. Thank you.'

The police arrived minutes later, two marked cars, each carrying two uniformed officers. They came through the door, flashlights blazing, and followed the direction in which I pointed.

'One deceased female, Caucasian,' I heard one say.

Another officer spoke into a handheld portable phone: 'We need detectives, lab technicians, the chief. We have a possible homicide.'

More cars arrived. Soon, there were six of them blocking the street. Their flashing lights and wailing sirens had awakened other residents, who stood outside their homes wearing robes and pajamas, their attention focused on the cottage behind yellow crime-scene tape that had been draped.

Inside Muller's cottage, the police forensic unit was hard at work in the bedroom. Hans

Muller sat in a corner of the living room with two detectives. Another detective was with me in the kitchen.

'Tell us again how you came to be here, Mrs. Fletcher,' the detective, whose name was Paul Kelley, asked. He was middle-aged, and wore a tan windbreaker over a maroon turtleneck. He had a youthful face and a warm smile.

I repeated everything I'd previously told him—about having been at a dinner party earlier with Jo Ann Forbes, our ride to Scott's Inn together, her decision to walk home, and the call at four A.M. from Hans Muller, informing me that Jo Ann was dead.

'What is your relationship with Mr. Muller?' he asked.

I shrugged. 'I don't have one really. I've met him a few times at dinner since arriving in the Hamptons. That about sums it up. I was with him at my publisher's house last night, and we were going to have dinner together tonight.'

I wished I hadn't mentioned the latter. It had no bearing on Jo Ann Forbes's death. All it did was cause Detective Kelley to raise his eyebrows and say, 'Sounds to me, Mrs. Fletcher, that your relationship with him, Mr. Muller, was—how shall I say? Growing?'

'Not at all.'

'Did Ms. Forbes and Mr. Muller have a relationship?'

'No. I mean, not that I know of.'

136

'You said she elected to walk home last night, and said she lived near here. Near where Muller lives.'

'That's right.'

'Looks like she walked here, rather than to where she lived.'

'It would seem that way.'

'Any ideas why she came here?'

'None whatsoever.'

'Well, Mrs. Fletcher, I'm sorry you had to be involved. Must have been a shock seeing this young woman only hours after she'd been alive and having a good time at a dinner party.'

'The shock was pretty much over once Mr. Muller made his call. Still—'

'Yeah, I know. Still—A ride back to Scott's Inn?'

'I'd appreciate that very much. What about Mr. Muller?'

'What about him?'

'I assume he's a suspect.'

'Sure. We'll have a lot more questions for him. In the meantime, thanks for your help. How long will you be in the Hamptons?'

'I'd planned on another week.'

'Good. There'll probably be loose ends I'll want to follow up on with you.'

'Anytime. By the way, Detective Kelley, do you know what funeral plans have been made for Miki Dorsey, the young model who died?'

'No, but I can find out. I'll call you.'

'I'd appreciate it.'

'That's right. You were there when she died—'

I smiled. 'You can say it. When she died, *too*.'

'Lousy coincidence for you.'

'Yes. Lousy coincidence.'

I intended to say good-bye to Hans Muller, but he was in the midst of his questioning by the two other detectives. He'd call, I knew. In the meantime I felt a desperate need for something to eat, and to get some sleep. I was dropped at the inn by a uniformed officer in one of the marked cars. Mr. Scott was sweeping the front porch when we arrived. He put down his broom and hurried down the path to where I was exiting the car.

'Mrs. Fletcher. Are you all right?'

'Fine, thank you, Mr. Scott. This officer was kind enough to give me a lift.'

'How is your sick friend?'

I couldn't meet his eyes. 'Not well,' I said.

'Anything else, Mrs. Fletcher?' the officer asked.

'No. You've been very kind. I'll be fine.'

Mr. Scott brought toast and tea to my room. Once I'd satisfied my gnawing hunger, I took a shower, got into fresh pajamas, climbed into bed, pulled the covers up under my chin, and tried to sleep away the memory of seeing Jo Ann Forbes dead on the floor of Hans Muller's bedroom. Detective Kelley had told me it appeared she'd been killed by a blow to the side of her head from a blunt object. An ambulance from a local hospital had arrived to take away her body as I was leaving. Another young death. Another autopsy.

I gave up any thoughts of sleeping. This vacationing writer of murder mysteries was undoubtedly in for a busy day, once the press learned I'd been close, yet again, to another death.

The only difference was that unlike Miki Dorsey, and the artist, Joshua Leopold, there was no debate about how Jo Ann Forbes had died. She'd been murdered, pure and simple.

And although I didn't have anything tangible to link those three deaths, I was certain there was a connection between them.

All I had to do was prove it.

CHAPTER FIFTEEN

Vaughan Buckley called:

'What in the world is going on, Jessica?' he asked the minute I picked up the phone.

'You've heard about Ms. Forbes.'

'Of course I have. Hans Muller called to tell me. You were there?'

'Yes. Not when she was killed. Muller called me and—it doesn't matter. It's horrible.'

'Hans says the police are treating him as though he's a suspect.'

'That's reasonable. She was found in his house. He says he found her. Did he say why he took so long to get home, Vaughan? He left your house at eleven-thirty. He didn't arrive at his cottage until four. Where was he?'

'He didn't mention that. How were you treated?'

'Fine. The detective who interviewed me was a perfect gentleman.'

'I'm glad to hear that. What are you doing today?'

'I haven't decided. I'd like to find out about Jo Ann's family. Another young life snuffed out.'

'Anything I can do to help?'

'Not that I can think of. But if I come up with something, I'll certainly ask.'

'Fair enough. Jess, Ms. Forbes's murder— and we know this one is murder—changes things. There's a murderer out there. And that means anyone close to these events is in potential danger.'

I didn't say anything.

'Did you hear me, Jess?'

'Yes, I heard you. And you're right. A little caution is in order from now on.'

'Glad to hear it from you. Keep in touch.'

Hans Muller called:

'Mrs. Fletcher, how are you?'

'All right, considering what's occurred. You?'

'Terrible. They question me as though I

140

killed Ms. Forbes.'

'Mr. Muller, did the detectives ask you where you'd been between the time you left the Buckleys' house, and when you arrived at your cottage?'

'*Ya*. They did.'

'I'm curious about that, too, Mr. Muller.'

It sounded again as though he were about to cry. 'Mr. Muller. Where were you?'

'I stopped to see a friend.'

'Oh? Who was that?'

'Mrs. Fletcher, why are you asking me such things? I answered questions by the police.'

'Because I had become friends with Ms. Forbes. And now she's dead. Murdered. In your house. I think I have every right to ask you that question.'

I could almost hear him stiffen. He said, 'I am surprised at you, Mrs. Fletcher, surprised, and offended at your—your—'

'I don't wish to offend, Mr. Muller, but receiving your call and seeing Jo Ann Forbes's body has been extremely upsetting, as anyone would understand.'

'I suppose—'

'Where were you?'

'Perhaps we can discuss it at dinner. That is, if the police do not lead me away in handcuffs.'

'Whether they do or not, Mr. Muller, I don't think I'm in the mood for dinner.'

'As you wish. You're a lovely woman, Mrs. Fletcher. And rude. *Guten tag*.'

141

'Good day to you, too, sir.'

The chief of police called:

'Mrs. Fletcher, this is Police Chief Cramer.'

'Hello, Chief Cramer.'

'I was wondering whether you'd be good enough to come to headquarters. Detective Kelley said you were extremely cooperative and helpful. I have some other questions that you might be able to answer.'

'I'll be happy to help in any way I can. When do you want me there?'

'Say an hour?'

'That's fine.' He told me where police headquarters was located, and we concluded the brief conversation.

The press, local and national, called.

Dr. Seth Hazlitt, my physician friend back in Cabot Cove, who'd heard on the radio that I'd been 'involved' in yet another death in the Hamptons, weighed in.

'Here you go again, Jessica, pokin' that pretty nose 'a yours into murder.'

'I wouldn't put it that way, Seth. Wrong place, wrong time, that's all.'

'I've heard that before. When are you comin' home?'

'As soon as my vacation is over.'

He laughed. 'As soon as you figure out who killed who, you mean.'

'If that should happen, Seth, you'll be the first to know. In Cabot Cove, that is. Have to run. Talk with you again soon.'

Cabot Cove Sheriff Morton Metzger, another good friend, also called after hearing the same news report. 'I just heard, Mrs. F., about what you're gettin' yourself into out there.'

'I'm not "out there," Mort. I'm down here, in the Hamptons, on the end of Long Island.'

'Wherever you are, doesn't sound to me like you're havin' much of a vacation.'

'Not true. I'm having a lovely time.'

'Trippin' over bodies isn't my idea of a vacation.'

'Mine, either. But I think I've seen the end of the bodies, Mort. It was good of you to call.'

'Always thinkin' about my favorite writer, Mrs. F. How's the art lessons cumin'?'

'On hold until I get home. I'll keep in touch. Love to everyone.'

The next call was one I eagerly took. It was from Scotland Yard Inspector George Sutherland.

'How are you, George?'

'Splendid, Jess. You?'

'I've been better.'

'Oh? What's happened?'

I filled him in on the events of early that morning. He listened with his usual patience. When I finished the story, he said, 'I don't like you being there. The mysterious death of the model was one thing. Now a murderer has shown his hand. You're too close to it, Jessica. I mean that.'

143

'I know you do, George, and I appreciate your concern. What did you come up with on poisons that mock heart attacks?'

He laughed. 'I fear my words fell on deaf ears.'

'Not at all. It's just that if I can come up with some answers—at least enough to satisfy this lady's insatiable curiosity—I'll be able to enjoy what time I have left on this vacation. And go back home with a clear mind.'

'I know you well enough, Jessica, to not waste too much time attempting to dissuade you. *Ricin.*'

'Pardon?'

'Ricin. A substance that fits your bill. One of the world's most toxic substances. Ranks right up there with botulinus. Let me see. I made notes while talking with my source, who, by the way, is an expert in such matters. Ricin is isolated from castor oil beans. It was considered as a possible chemical warfare agent in World War Two. Thank God cooler heads prevailed. My friend tells me that one-millionth of a gram is enough to kill thousands of people. As many as fifty thousand.'

'My goodness.'

'Shocking, I'd say.'

'What about it causing a medical examiner to think death might have resulted from natural causes? Say, a heart attack.'

'Ricin is very hard to detect in a body, Jess, especially because it takes only such a tiny

144

amount to kill. Most medical examiners miss it because they're not even aware of its existence. They don't look for such an exotic agent. It would take an especially keen examiner, one who would include ricin on his or her list of things to look for, to identify it as a possible cause of death.'

'I see,' I said. 'How is ricin administered?'

'I asked that question, too. Evidently, it can be ingested, inhaled, or injected. A versatile murder weapon, wouldn't you say?'

'Yes.'

'You say this latest young person to die, this Ms. Forbes, was killed by a blow to the head. If something like ricin was used to kill the young model—Ms. Dorsey, is it?—it seems unlikely that the murderer would so dramatically shift *modus operandi*. In one case, he or she utilizes one of the most exotic substances known to man. In the next, brute force is used.'

'I agree,' I said. 'But maybe two different murderers are involved. George, how would someone not involved in clandestine government agencies get hold of something like ricin?'

'Hard to say. But we all know how even the most protected of things, whether it's poison or documents or anything else, often end up in unintended hands. Dangerous hands.'

'Unfortunately, you're right.'

'What do you intend to do with the information I've given you, Jessica?'

'I don't know. I'll think of something. Thanks so much, George, for taking the time to come up with this.'

'More important, Jess, when will I see you again?'

I smiled. He never failed to ask that, no matter what the genesis of our conversations.

'Soon, I hope.' It was my usual stock answer when I didn't have a better one.

'Characteristically vague, as usual. But I'll pin you down, Jessica. I always get my man. Or in this case, woman.'

'George, any further information you can give me on Blaine Dorsey?'

'Not really. As I told you, he's got a shady reputation in the London art world. Was a suspect in a murder a few years ago, never formally charged. Chatted with one of our art squad detectives about Dorsey. The claim was that this young artist was killed in order to boost the prices of his artwork.'

'Good Lord, George. Someone would actually do that?'

'Nothing surprises me anymore, Jess. Not in this world. Actually, it turned out that the artist was killed by someone to shut him up about a counterfeiting ring. Painting copies of valuable art.'

'Amazing, what people will do for money. Well, thank you again, George, for your help. I'll be in touch.'

'Sooner, rather than later, I hope.'

'Sooner. I promise.'

I'd made notes of what George had said about this powerful poison, ricin. Reading them caused me to shudder, and to feel a sudden chill. What horrible things we human beings have invented to kill fellow human beings.

Police Chief Cramer had said his office was within walking distance of Scott's Inn. A knot of reporters milled about on the porch as I came through the door. They started shooting questions at me, but I waved them off with a smile and set out at a brisk pace, with them falling in behind. It was a lovely day, sunny and with a crispness in the air to which I always respond.

They asked repeatedly where I was going. When I walked up the steps to police headquarters, they had their answer. I stopped before entering, turned, and said, 'I know you're doing your job, but—'

'Except,' a young man interrupted, 'Jo Ann Forbes was one of us. A journalist.'

I had to nod. He was right. For them, there was more to her murder than there might have been under other circumstances.

'Look,' I said, 'I'm sorry about what happened to Jo Ann Forbes. She'd become my friend. I hated being called to go see her body at the cottage, and I'm determined to—'

I hadn't meant to publicly announce that I was interested in finding out who'd murdered

147

Jo Ann, and perhaps link her death to Miki Dorsey's and—and I knew this was a long shot—and maybe even find a connection to the death of Joshua Leopold, the young artist who, like Miki, had allegedly died of a premature heart attack.

'You're determined to *what*, Mrs. Fletcher?'

'To—to help the authorities in any way I can. Please excuse me. I have an appointment inside.'

'With the police?'

I entered the building and asked a uniformed woman at a desk for Chief Cramer.

'Yes, Mrs. Fletcher. Down that hall. Last door on the right.'

For some reason—I suppose it's because I spend most of my life in a small Maine town called Cabot Cove—I expect the police of similar small towns to be, well, not especially military. Mort Metzger, Cabot Cove's police chief, is a good-looking man who isn't exactly what you'd call in shape.

But Chief Cramer was straight out of a West Point recruitment flyer. Salt-and-pepper hair was closely cropped, almost a crew cut. He was slender, and wore his uniform, replete with medals, as though standing inspection at a military base. He smiled broadly, extended his hand, and said, 'It's a pleasure meeting you, Mrs. Fletcher. Thanks for coming.'

'It would never have occurred to me not to heed your call.'

I sat across the desk from him. He leaned his elbows on it and said, 'Tough night for you.'

'Worse than that, I'm afraid.'

'Detective Kelley filled me in on what you told him at Mr. Muller's cottage. Frankly, what you said raised other questions for me.'

'Such as?'

'Why Muller called *you*.'

'He told me it was my number that first came to his mind.'

'He had your number?'

'He knew I was staying at Scott's Inn. We were to have dinner together tonight. He was to call to arrange a time and place.'

'Okay. What do you know about Muller?'

I shrugged. 'Not much.' I explained my two brief meetings with him. 'He called me this morning. He's upset that he's considered a suspect.'

Cramer sat back and smiled. 'What does he expect? A girl is found murdered in the bedroom of his cottage.'

'Chief Cramer, did Mr. Muller explain where he'd been between the time he left the dinner party at the Buckleys, and arriving home at four in the morning?'

'Sure.'

'What did he say?'

The chief consulted notes on his desk. 'He said he was with a friend, Blaine Dorsey.'

I sat up straight. 'The father of the young

149

model, Miki Dorsey, who died a few days ago.'

'One and the same, Mrs. Fletcher. Muller said he stopped in to see Dorsey at his hotel.'

'A late visit,' I said.

'That's right, only late nights aren't unusual here in the Hamptons. Lots of late parties. The rich tend to stay up late and sleep late.'

I smiled. 'I'm afraid I'm not one of them.'

'Me, either. I hear around town that you question how Miki Dorsey died.'

I shook my head. 'I'm not questioning it exactly, Chief Cramer. Did you know the artist, Joshua Leopold?'

'Yes. He died, too, of—of a heart attack—at a very young age.'

My eyebrows went up. 'Raise any questions with you?'

'No. But to be honest, I hadn't thought of Leopold in connection with Ms. Dorsey's death. You aren't suggesting that both were killed, are you?'

'Just asking, that's all. Just playing the "what if" game.'

Cramer smiled. 'The mystery writer's mind at work.'

'Something like that. I was told Miki Dorsey owned an original Joshua Leopold painting, and that it disappeared from her room after she died.'

'That's news to me. The only missing art I've heard about is your sketch of the—'

I completed his sentence: 'Of the naked

male model. Is finding it on your agenda?'

'Of course.' He stood and went to the window, arched his back against a stiffness, turned, and said, 'Mrs. Fletcher, I'll be up front with you. Your suspicions about everything not being what they seem might not be far-fetched.'

'Oh?'

'I can't tell you my sources, but there's some speculation that Jo Ann Forbes might have been killed because of the artist, Joshua Leopold. And if Miki Dorsey didn't die of a heart attack, she, too, could have been killed over the same issue.'

'The coroner said it was a heart attack.'

'I know. But because there is this—how shall I put it?—this *possibility* of a link between Jo Ann Forbes's murder, and the death of the other two, we're holding Ms. Dorsey's body. Her father is pretty upset over it, claims he wants to have her buried immediately in England. He's threatening legal action.'

'Can he win such an action?'

'Not in time to make much difference. Know anything about art, aside from doing some painting of your own?'

'Very little.'

'People kill other people over paintings.'

'Some paintings are worth millions,' I said.

'Worth killing for. This Leopold, his works command big bucks, I understand.'

'That's true. Chief Cramer, you asked me

here to answer some questions. I really haven't heard many.'

'Guilty as charged, Mrs. Fletcher. I got you here under false pretenses. I'd like your help.'

'That's not a problem. But I don't think I have much help to give.'

'Too modest, Mrs. Fletcher. Let me cite two things. One, you have a reputation as a remarkably astute detective. And two—'

'Chief Cramer, I might write about solving crimes, but I'm a rank amateur when it comes to actually doing it.'

'Not from what I hear. Two, you seem to be in the thick of things here when it comes to people dying, and art. You know this Hans Muller. You were the person he called regarding Ms. Forbes. You were there when Ms. Dorsey died. You've been to Ms. Dorsey's house, met her father. You seem to know a great deal about the artist, Joshua Leopold. I'd say you're in a position to be of immeasurable help to me.'

'As I said, I'll be happy to do what I can.'

'Mean that?'

'Of course. Just call.'

'I will. Buy you a cup of coffee?'

'Thanks, no. I have things to do. What funeral plans have been made for Jo Ann Forbes?'

'None yet. Another autopsy to be performed. Her folks have been notified. They're coming in from Baltimore. Hell of a

152

reason to make a trip.'

'The worst I can imagine.'

CHAPTER SIXTEEN

Reporters were waiting for me outside. I wasn't sure what to do next, aside from getting away from them. I looked across the street and saw there was a tiny white building with a sign that read Taxi. I quickly crossed and entered the building, where a little old man, wearing a baseball cap and a yellow cable-knit sweater that had seen better days, sat behind a desk reading a magazine.

'Good morning,' I said.

He looked up. 'Good morning. Something I can do for you?'

'Yes. I need a taxi.'

'No problem.' He tossed the magazine on the desk and stood. 'Where to?'

'Many places. I need a taxi for about a week.'

He looked at me quizzically.

'I need a car and a driver for a week,' I said. 'I'm here on vacation.'

'Happy to oblige, lady, but you'd do better—be cheaper to rent a car.'

'I don't drive.'

'Oh. Well, in that case, I suppose we can work something out.'

'That's good to hear.'

Fifteen minutes later I was in the backseat of an older blue sedan, with Mr. Fred Mayer, owner of Fred's Taxi Service, at the wheel. He'd called a friend to take over the day-to-day operation of his taxi business, and committed himself to me for the duration. I liked Fred Mayer. He had a wry sense of humor, not unlike some of my friends back home, and would surely prove to be a valuable source of insider gossip about the Hamptons and its summer residents.

I looked back; the press stood on the sidewalk. I felt better.

I gave Mr. Mayer the address of the sprawling old waterfront house in which Miki Dorsey had lived before her death. We pulled into the driveway and stopped. Mayer turned. 'Here we are, Mrs. Fletcher.'

'Fine. You'll wait, of course.'

He smiled. 'I'm yours for the day. For the next seven days. That's the deal.'

I knocked on the front door. When no one replied, I tentatively opened it. 'Hello?'

'Hello' came a male voice from somewhere in the house.

I stepped inside, closed the door, and headed down the hall I knew led to the large living room. Chris Turi, whom I'd met on the jitney, and who was said to have been Miki Dorsey's love interest, was seated on a window seat by a window overlooking the ocean.

'Hello, Mrs. Fletcher,' he said.

'Hello, Chris. Hope you don't mind my barging in unannounced like this.'

'No. How are you?'

Since he didn't get up, I went to him. 'I'm not very good, to be honest. You heard, I assume, about the reporter, Jo Ann Forbes.'

At least I'd gotten his attention. He sat up and said, 'No. What about her?'

'Did you know her?'

'No. Well, maybe I met her at a party or something.'

'She was murdered this morning.'

'Huh?'

'She was murdered early this morning. Not far from here, as a matter of fact.'

'I didn't know that.'

'Sorry to be the bearer of the news. Chris, do you think I could see Miki's room?'

He frowned. 'I suppose so. But why?'

'Just curious. I feel a certain kinship with her. I suppose it's because I was there when she died.'

'Yeah. I can understand that. Actually, I've—well, once the police were through checking out her room, I sort of moved in. It's bigger than mine was and—'

'No need to explain. Have all of Miki's things been moved?'

'Yes. I mean, out. They're in a storage room. Her father says he'll arrange for them to go back with him to England.'

'Has he been here much?'

Turi shook his head. 'Come on, I'll show you the room. But excuse the mess. I'm still getting settled.'

The room was at the other end of the rear of the house. The door was open, and Turi indicated with his hand that I should enter. It hadn't been an overstatement; the room was in chaos. Clothing was tossed into every corner. Books from piles had toppled to the floor. The bed was unmade. The blinds were crooked. Pictures on the walls had obviously been hung haphazardly and at cockeyed angles. I thought of the movie *Rocky,* and Burgess Meredith's line when he first saw Rocky's hovel: 'Nice place you got here.' I didn't say it.

I stood in the middle of the room and felt a profound sadness. This was where Miki Dorsey read, and slept, and thought about her life and where she wanted it to go.

I turned and said to Chris Turi, 'Do you know anything about a painting missing from Miki's room?'

He didn't seem comfortable answering, so I asked again.

'The Leopold.'

'You do know about it.'

'I heard.'

'My understanding is that it hung right here in her room. Do you remember seeing it?'

He shrugged, and looked even more uncomfortable. 'I guess I did. I never paid

156

attention.'

I shifted my attention to the paintings on the walls. 'Are these yours, Chris?'

'Yeah. Are you hungry? Can I get you something?'

'No thank you. Your work is very good.'

What struck me about them was their similarity to the Joshua Leopold painting style. To my untrained eye, they could almost have been interchangeable to some of Leopold's paintings in Maurice St. James's gallery.

'Did you know Joshua Leopold?' I asked.

'Who? Oh, Leopold. No.'

'Never met him?'

'No. Look, I—'

'I ask because your style strikes me as being influenced by him.'

'Nah. Pollock, maybe. Lichtenstein. Kandinsky. I like Kandinsky a lot. And Masson.'

'I don't know him.'

'He brought the viewer into the unconscious. Done here, Mrs. Fletcher?'

'Yes. Thanks for showing it to me.'

We stood in the kitchen, where Turi made himself a sandwich. I accepted a diet drink from him. As he spread mayonnaise on his bread, he asked, 'How was the reporter murdered?'

'Someone hit her head very hard.'

'You said it happened not far from here.'

'That's right. At a beach cottage rented by a

German art collector, Hans Muller.'

He dropped the knife to the floor, hurriedly picked it up, and wiped the resulting mayo spill with a paper towel.

'I take it you know Mr. Muller,' I said, following him to the window seat. He sat and started to eat.

'I've heard of him. It happened at Hans's— *his* cottage?'

'That's right. Well, Chris, you've been very gracious. Thanks for the soft drink. It was refreshing.'

'Sure. Anytime, Mrs. Fletcher.'

He didn't make a move to escort me to the front door, so I started on my own. Before I left, I turned and said, 'When we met in the pizza parlor, I said Anne Harris told me you and Miki were close. You denied it. Were you?'

'What do you mean, "close"?'

I smiled. 'Chris, I think you know full well what I mean.'

'Did we sleep together? Sure. Big deal. Welcome to the nineties, Mrs. Fletcher.'

I chewed my cheek. 'I've heard that the pendulum has swung into the nineties, Chris. But you've answered my question, thank you. Hope to see you again.'

Fred Mayer jumped out of his cab and opened the door for me. 'No need for that, Mr. Mayer,' I said. 'But thanks anyway.'

'Where to now?' Mayer asked, starting the

158

engine.

I checked my watch. A little after eleven. I knew I should have been tired, considering I'd been up since four. But I wasn't. I was energized. The problem was I didn't know what to do next with my energy.

'Feel like a tour?' Mayer asked.

'A tour. That sounds wonderful. I really haven't seen much of the Hamptons.'

We drove along narrow country roads, coming close to water, leaving it, skirting marshland, passing lovely homes large and small, then back at the water, quiet bay beaches that reminded me of Cabot Cove, old inns and ultramodern houses. There were lots of bike riders, which caused me to reconsider my decision to hire Fred Mayer to drive me. I often ride my bicycle at home and love it. But I rationalized my decision based upon a lack of time. When I ride my bike, I like to do it leisurely, without a need to be somewhere quickly. As appealing as getting on a bike in the Hamptons was, Fred Mayer made more sense.

After forty-five minutes, Mayer asked if there was anything I especially wanted to see.

'A restaurant,' I said. 'I'm hungry. But first, would you drop me off at Scott's Inn. I need to pick up something.'

'Sure thing. That's a nice place to stay. Joe Scott's a real gentleman.'

'He certainly is. And he runs a very good

hotel.'

As I walked through the door to the inn, I was surprised to see Vaughan Buckley in the small library, browsing in one of my books he'd taken from the shelf.

'Vaughan. What are you doing here?'

He replaced the book, shook his head, and motioned for me to sit down in a small upholstered chair in the corner. He sat in a matching chair at my side. 'Hoping you'd return,' he said.

'Is something wrong?'

'Yes. I'd say there is. Hans Muller arrived at the house right after I talked to you.'

'And?'

'He was beside himself. Of course, it doesn't take a lot to send him off the deep end.'

'Has he been accused of Jo Ann Forbes's murder?'

'Not officially. But they're holding his passport.'

'Somehow, Vaughan, I don't think you're here because your chain-smoking German friend lost his passport.'

'You're right, Jess. It's what *else* he lost that brings me here.'

'What was that?'

'The painting he took from the house last night. You know, the modern work he wanted to examine.'

'He's *lost* it?'

'That's what he says. Jess, when you were

160

called to his cottage, did you see that painting?'

'No. But then again, I wasn't looking at anything except Ms. Forbes's body. When Mr. Muller left your house after the party, he stopped in to see Blaine Dorsey at Dorsey's hotel.'

'The dead model's father?'

'Yes.'

'How did you learn that?'

'Police Chief Cramer.'

'When did you talk to him?'

'This morning. Vaughan, were you being truthful when you said you didn't know the artist who'd done that painting?'

'Between you and me?'

'Sure.'

'Olga and I think it's a Joshua Leopold. An early work. That's the only reason I allowed Hans to take it. He's a Leopold expert.'

'So is Blaine Dorsey.'

'Maybe he took it to Dorsey for his opinion.'

'A good possibility. But now it's lost, you say.'

'That's what Hans says. He claims he took it with him to his cottage, found Ms. Forbes, called you, and waited for the police. Then, he says, after everyone left, the painting was gone.'

'I'm sorry.'

'It's not the painting that upsets me, Jess, although it does represent a possible substantial loss. The problem is that I don't believe Hans.'

'About the painting simply disappearing?'

'Right. And once you don't believe a friend about one thing, it's hard to believe him about others.'

'Like Jo Ann Forbes's murder.'

'Exactly. Jess, stay away from Hans.'

My laugh was small. 'I've already come to that conclusion on my own. We were to have dinner tonight. I canceled.'

'Good.'

'Vaughan, tell me what you know about Hans Muller, his life, his background.'

'I don't know much. He's East German, worked for one of its agencies until the Wall came down.'

'What agency?'

Vaughan laughed. 'Some clandestine agency, to hear him tell it. Like a KGB or CIA. From what I've heard, he was in a position to smuggle out of East Germany a lot of expensive art. But you can't prove it by me.'

'Interesting.'

'He's an interesting man, despite those infernal cigarettes and his penchant for too much whiskey.'

He glanced out the window. 'That cab waiting for you?'

'Yes. I booked him for a week.'

'Jess, why didn't you call me. I could have arranged for a limo and driver.'

'I don't need a limousine, Vaughan. Mr. Mayer is charming, and knows a lot about the Hamptons. I'm perfectly happy with him.'

'You can be—frustrating.'

'My Scottish friend, George Sutherland, says the same thing. I'll keep my eye open for your painting. And you can do the same where my sketch is concerned.'

'I almost forgot. A friend told me your sketch is now being offered for three thousand.'

'Three thousand?' I couldn't help but laugh loudly.

'Name value. Dinner tonight?'

'Love it. Call me later.'

CHAPTER SEVENTEEN

I went to my room and sat in an overstuffed chair by the window. I needed a few minutes of relax time. The trauma of that morning was catching up with me, and I didn't want to allow that. If I totally let down, I was afraid I'd spend the rest of the day and night with nothing on my brain but the gruesome vision of Jo Ann Forbes wedged between the bed and wall of Hans Muller's cottage.

I freshened up and returned to where Fred Mayer waited in his cab. I'd made a decision on my way down. I wanted to touch base with

Jo Ann Forbes's parents—if I could find them. Police Chief Cramer said they were on their way to the Hamptons from Baltimore.

'Next stop?' asked Mayer.

'Police headquarters, if you don't mind.'

'Thought you were hungry.'

'Hungry for information,' I said. 'I'll eat after police headquarters. Have a good restaurant to recommend?'

'I will by the time you're ready, Mrs. Fletcher.'

Chief Cramer wasn't at headquarters, but I was introduced to his deputy, a young woman named Gloria Watson, sharply dressed in her close-fitting brown uniform, her short-cropped red hair as precise as Chief Cramer's.

'I was with the chief earlier,' I told her.

'I know, Mrs. Fletcher. He told me. Can I help you?'

'I was wondering whether Ms. Forbes's parents have arrived yet. Chief Cramer said they were coming from Baltimore.'

'They got here only ten minutes ago. They flew to Kennedy, and took a private plane out of there to Spadaro's Airport.'

'They must be devastated.'

'Surprisingly calm, Mrs. Fletcher. Maybe that's not the right word. But they are in control of themselves. They mentioned you.'

'They did?'

'Yes. Evidently, Ms. Forbes kept in very close touch with them. She told them during phone conversations that she'd met you and was—'

A door opened and a middle-aged man and woman looked at us. Deputy Watson glanced at me, then at them. She seemed unsure of what to do.

The woman, who was short and chunky, locked eyes with me. 'Jessica Fletcher?'

'Yes.'

'Mrs. Fletcher, this is Mr. and Mrs. Forbes,' Deputy Watson said.

'I'm so sorry about your daughter,' I said.

Mrs. Forbes tried to force a smile, which immediately degenerated into tears. Her considerably taller husband put his arm around her. I fought back my own tears.

'This is not the time for us to meet,' I said. 'Perhaps another time.'

'No,' Mrs. Forbes said. 'Please, stay, Mrs. Fletcher. Jo Ann was thrilled at meeting you. She said you and she were becoming friends, and that you'd offered to help her with her stories.'

'That's true,' I said. 'She was a lovely young woman, and I suspect a very good reporter.'

Mrs. Forbes swallowed hard, again supported by her husband.

'Would you like to sit?' Deputy Watson asked, indicating the room in which Mr. and Mrs. Forbes stood. I looked past them to see a good-size room containing a conference table and chairs.

'Please,' said Mr. Forbes. He extended his hand. 'I'm Bob Forbes. This is my wife, Mary.'

Deputy Watson closed the door behind us as we took seats at the pine table. I was uncomfortable; what can you say except 'I'm sorry for your loss'?

But Bob Forbes put me at ease by saying, 'I know how awkward this must be for you, Mrs. Fletcher.'

What a remarkable man, I thought. Jo Ann Forbes came from good stock. 'Yes,' I said. 'It is. Please call me Jessica.'

'I suppose you can say that Mary and I are pragmatists. That doesn't alleviate the pain of losing Jo Ann, especially considering the violent nature of her death. But she taught us a lot.'

'She taught you?'

'Yes. She had this fatalistic view of life. You take chances, you take risks. And if you're not lucky, you can get hurt.'

'Quite a sophisticated philosophy,' I said.

'She was a very sophisticated young woman,' said Mary Forbes. 'She had such ambition as a journalist. She saw the art story she was working on as a possible launching pad to a job with a big newspaper, maybe even television. She always said she wanted to work on *Sixty Minutes*.' She wept softly and her husband covered her hand on the table with one of his.

'Have you heard anything, Mrs. Fletcher,

about who might have murdered our daughter?' Bob Forbes asked.

'Sorry to say that I haven't. You mentioned a story Jo Ann was working on about art.'

'Yes,' her father replied. 'The one she said you were helping her with.'

'I'm afraid not much of a story has developed with that,' I said. 'It had to do with a young model's death from natural causes.'

'She told us that. But she said you weren't convinced that it was natural causes.'

'Just a hunch on my part, Mr. Forbes.'

'Bob. And Mary.'

'Of course. Bob, was Jo Ann looking into that story beyond the model's death?'

His eyebrows went up. 'Yes. I assumed you knew.'

'I'm afraid I don't know more than what I've told you, except my question about the model's death—her name was Miki Dorsey— seems to be on the minds of a few other people.'

'The missing painting.' Mary Forbes said it so softly and flatly that I barely heard her.

'What missing painting?'

'The one you and Jo Ann were trying to find.'

'Oh, *that* missing art. My sketch.'

'Your sketch?' said Bob Forbes. 'Jo Ann didn't say anything about that. She said she'd learned that paintings by some artist here in the Hamptons—his name was Leopard or Leonard, or something like that—were missing.'

'Leopold,' I offered. 'Joshua Leopold.'

'That's it.'

'Was your daughter talking about a painting allegedly missing from the dead model's room?'

Bob and Mary Forbes looked at each other, their expressions quizzical. Mary Forbes answered: 'No, I don't think so. Jo Ann said—what term did she use, Bob?—she said there was an underground market for this artist's paintings. People were stealing them. Wasn't that what Jo Ann said, Bob?'

'Exactly.' He smiled. 'Of course, when Jo Ann was excited about something she was working on, she talked fast. Full of enthusiasm. She—'

Mary Forbes broke down. Bob Forbes wrapped his arms around her and held her tight.

I was glad when the door behind me opened and Deputy Watson, along with Chief Cramer, entered the room.

'Hello again, Mrs. Fletcher,' Cramer said.

I stood. 'I was just leaving, Chief.'

Bob Forbes stood, too. 'Any word on who did this, Chief Cramer?'

'Not yet, but we'll get to the bottom of it, Mr. Forbes. I'm afraid you're going to have to identify your daughter's body. I know, I know. It's a brutal thing to go through. But it must be done.'

'I'll go,' Bob Forbes said. 'You stay here, Mary, with Mrs. Fletcher. If you don't mind staying a little longer,' he said to me.

'Of course I'll stay,' I said.

But Mary Forbes got up, took her husband's hand, and looked up into his eyes. 'We'll go together,' she said.

Deputy Gloria Watson and I were alone in the room.

'Have the police been to Ms. Forbes's house yet?' I asked.

'Yes. We sent a squad immediately. They've secured it. Detectives are there now going through her things.'

'Where did she live?'

Watson opened a file folder and read Jo Ann's address.

'When will her parents be allowed to go there to gather her belongings?'

'Up to the chief. Whenever the detectives are finished.'

'I'd like to go there.'

'You would?'

'Yes. Do you think Chief Cramer would allow me?'

'It's up to him.'

'And Mr. and Mrs. Forbes.'

'Ask them.'

The return of Bob and Mary Forbes and Chief Cramer was wrenching. Mary sobbed, and her husband, tears running down his cheeks, tried to comfort her. I liked these folks. They were decent and caring, and strong. Good people, like many of my friends and neighbors back in Cabot Cove.

Eventually, without anyone saying anything, they regained their composure and asked if they could go to their daughter's house. Chief Cramer went to his office, returned minutes later to say, 'The detectives have finished up there. We can go now if you'd like.'

I was poised to ask whether I could accompany them, but Bob Forbes saved me the question. 'Would you like to come with us, Mrs. Fletcher? Jessica?'

'Yes.'

Chief Cramer and his deputy, Gloria Watson, transported Bob and Mary Forbes in his marked car. Fred Mayer and I followed by Mayer's taxi.

Jo Ann Forbes had lived in a pretty pale green house a few blocks from one of the bays. It was a small home, but obviously well kept. The postage-stamp patch of lawn in front was manicured, a virtual putting green. The paint was fresh, as were flowers in window boxes and in hanging baskets.

We stood just inside yellow crime-scene tape that had been strung. A uniformed officer stood at the front door.

'Had you been here before?' I asked.

'Yes,' Jo Ann's father answered. 'Right after Jo Ann took the job at *Dan's Papers* and moved to the Hamptons. We helped her get settled.'

'And we visited two weeks ago,' said Mary Forbes. 'We had such fun.'

'Let's go in,' Cramer said, sensing that to stand there talking about the deceased girl would only generate more sorrow and tears.

The inside was as pristine as the outside. The wood floors glistened with polish. Starched white curtains fluttered in a breeze through open windows. The furniture was old, and comfortable. Everything was as neat as a pin. I wasn't surprised.

'My detectives didn't find anything they felt would help shed light on what happened,' Chief Cramer said. 'Feel free to go where you want.'

Jo Ann's parents stood in the middle of the living room, as though unsure what to do and which direction to take. I felt it best to leave them alone, and slowly wandered into the kitchen. Clean dishes were in a dish drainer on the sink. A large bird feeder just outside a window was doing a landslide business.

I peeked into a small room that served as a pantry. A door from it led to the backyard. Mr. and Mrs. Forbes joined me.

'Everything's so neat,' I said.

'That's the way she was,' said her father.

I left them and went up a narrow set of stairs to the second floor, where two bedrooms were located. One had been turned into an office. I stepped into it and perused what was on her desk. Nothing caught my eye. I sat and opened the right-hand drawer, which had been configured to accommodate hanging files. They were segregated into three sections, each using different-color folders. Those in front were red; the middle section was yellow; the section to the back of the drawer contained green folders. Jo Ann Forbes, among other attributes, was a highly organized young lady.

I started through the front red files. They seemed to be reserved for personal matters: papers regarding her 1994 Mazda automobile, health insurance, investments, taxes for the previous year, credit-card receipts, personal receipts.

The yellow files in the middle held folders marked 'Research.' Jo Ann obviously had clipped items from newspapers and magazines that she felt might be grist for future stories under her byline. There were also numerous scraps of paper on which she'd noted her reactions to the clippings, as well as independent story ideas that had occurred to her.

The rear section of the drawer, with its green files, was the repository for Jo Ann's files on stories she was working on for *Dan's Papers*, along with other files containing material relating to potential stories based upon information she'd gathered in the Hamptons. One hanging file folder tab immediately caught my eye: LEOPOLD,

JOSHUA.

I was in the process of pulling out that folder when Chief Cramer end Deputy Watson entered the room. 'Find anything interesting, Mrs. Fletcher?' Cramer asked.

'Not really. She was so well organized. I was just perusing some of her files.'

'And?'

'She kept this file on the artist, Joshua Leopold. I was just about to see what was in it.'

Mr. and Mrs. Forbes came up the stairs and joined us. Seeing them reminded me that I was overstepping my bounds, poking through their deceased daughters's papers and files. I asked them directly if they minded my doing that.

'Not at all,' Bob Forbes replied. 'Jo Ann told us during our last phone conversation that she had tremendous faith in you. So do we. Please feel free to look at anything you'd like.'

'Thank you,' I said. My admiration for them grew with each passing minute.

Deputy Watson went with the Forbeses to Jo Ann's bedroom. Chief Cramer pulled up a chair next to me as I opened the folder marked LEOPOLD, JOSHUA, and began reviewing what was in it, handing each sheet to the chief as I finished reading it. We'd gone through a half-dozen sheets of paper when I started reading the seventh, and let out a small, involuntary grunt.

Cramer said, 'Find something, Mrs. Fletcher?'

I finished reading, then handed it to him. 'I find this fascinating,' I said.

He frowned as he read. When he was through, he handed the paper back, saying, 'I see what you mean.'

The paper, page one of three, contained Jo Ann's notes on what she'd uncovered about Leopold's career, his output—which, according to her, was prodigious—and some observations on his sudden death a year ago, allegedly because of a heart attack.

There were two additional pages, extensions of the first page, which I read and gave to Chief Cramer.

'Is that it?' he asked.

'Yes.'

'So, Mrs. Fletcher, give me your read on these pages.'

'I want to read them again. I wonder—' I looked to a corner where there was a small photocopy machine. 'Mind if I make a copy?' I asked.

'Not if you make two.'

I copied the three pages and replaced the originals in the file. 'I have a suggestion,' I said.

'What's that?'

'That we both read these pages, then get together for some joint analysis of them.'

'Makes sense to me.'

'Just as long as we make sense out of these pieces of paper.'

174

'Need a ride back to Scott's Inn?'

'No, thanks. I have Mr. Mayer for the day. For the week, as a matter of fact.'

Cramer smiled. 'A nice old fella,' he said. 'But keep him away from restaurants and bars. He's been known to down a few.'

'And drive a cab?'

'Seldom at the same time. When do you want to get together again?'

'Tomorrow? In the morning? Say ten?'

'I'll come to you this time, Mrs. Fletcher. Scott's Inn at ten.'

CHAPTER EIGHTEEN

'Hungry now?' Fred Mayer asked after I'd climbed into the backseat of his taxi.

'Yes, but it's too late for lunch. I'll be having dinner soon.' It suddenly dawned on me that he hadn't had lunch, either, and I asked if he'd like to stop for something.

'Snuck a sandwich while you were inside,' he replied.

'Good. Mr. Mayer, do you remember back a year ago when a young artist named Joshua Leopold died?'

'Sure do. I drove lots of folks to his studio, where he died.'

'Excellent.'

'Still an artist's studio, I think. Different

175

artists, though.'

'Can we go there?'

'On our way.'

The studio in which artist Joshua Leopold had worked, and died, was typical of so many other small buildings in the Hamptons. It was close to the town dock, where I'd ended up after my garage sale expedition. Its white clapboard was stained with black and green streaks; scraggly grass grew in clumps along a front walk of cracked and chipped flagstone.

There was a small sign next to the door, too small to read from the cab. 'Back in a minute,' I said, exiting and going to the door.

The crude sign read W-T STUDIOS. I'd just read it when the door opened, and a young woman faced me. 'Can I help you?' she asked.

She startled me: 'No. Ah, yes. This is an artist's studio, isn't it?'

She smiled sweetly. 'Yes it is. Want to come in?'

'Thank you.' I looked back at Fred Mayer, who appeared to be dozing behind the wheel.

The building consisted of one large room, which had been partitioned into four areas. The two spaces to the rear had easels. Paintings in various stages of completion were tacked up everywhere.

The space to my left was obviously occupied by a sculptor. To the right, a potter's tools were evident.

'Are things here for sale?' I asked. 'Or is it

176

just a working space?'

'Both. Look around. I was just putting up a fresh pot of coffee. Like some?'

'That would be lovely, thank you.'

She attended to a coffeemaker in what I judged was her space—she was the sculptor—and I browsed, eventually ending up in one of the artist's spaces at the back of the room. I looked at the paintings pinned up to the wall, crude watercolor renderings of naked men and women.

I moved to the other space. Remarkable, I thought. These recently rendered works looked like they'd come from the brush and palette of Joshua Leopold. And one, of a nude young woman, looked strangely like Miki Dorsey. Not the face. Everything in the painting was too obscured by energetic brush strokes and slashes of vivid color from a palette knife. But it was the pose that captured my attention. Within the abstraction was a young woman seated on a stool, her head hung down low between her knees. It could have been Miki. What reality the artist had injected into the work showed a body structured very much like I remembered her body to be.

'How do you take it?'

I turned. The young woman was standing just behind me. 'Your coffee,' she said.

'Black will be fine.'

She handed me a steaming mug.

'Who are these artists?' I asked, taking a sip.

'Chris and Carlton. They're not here, but should be back in about an hour.'

'Chris Turi and Carlton Wells?'

She laughed. 'I see you know your art, and artists. Have you met them before?'

'No. Maybe in passing. But I certainly know their work.'

'That's always nice for an artist to hear. Well, I have to get back to something I'm working on. Make yourself at home.' She extended her hand. 'I'm Debbie Lane.'

I shook her hand and mumbled my name.

'Fletcher, you say?'

'That's right.'

'Give a yell if you need anything.'

Carlton Wells, my instructor, and Chris Turi sharing a studio. Well, well.

Both had had an intimate relationship with Miki Dorsey.

Everyone I talked to, it seemed, considered Wells to be a swine of sorts.

Chris Turi had showed no remorse over Miki's death.

What was going on here?

I lingered in Chris Turi's space. As I did, the similarity of his painting style to Joshua Leopold became more striking. I was about to leave when my eye went to a small table on which jars of paint stood. Among them was an open package of cigarettes. I glanced back to see if Debbie Lane was looking. She wasn't; she was focused on a small piece of marble

178

being transformed into some sort of figure.

I picked up the pack, pulled out a cigarette, and examined it closely. I wasn't sure, but it appeared to me to be similar to the butt I'd picked up just outside where Miki Dorsey died, and from beside the tree in the garden behind Scott's Inn. I put the cigarette in the pocket of the light teal windbreaker I wore and emerged from Turi's space.

'Ms. Lane, is this the studio where Joshua Leopold died?' I asked, coming abreast of her working space.

She looked up. 'Yes, it is.'

'What a tragedy that was,' I said. 'So talented, and so young.'

'Sure was. I didn't know him. I just started renting this space a month ago from Chris and Carlton. It's my first season out here in the Hamptons.'

'Oh? Where are you from?'

'The city. Do you live here year-round?'

'No. Just visiting. Do Chris Turi and Carlton Wells ever talk about Josh Leopold?'

'No. I don't think so. There's a gallery in town that features his work.'

'I know. I've been there. It's owned by a gentleman named St. James. Maurice St. James.'

'I don't know who owns it. Do you want to leave a number where Chris or Carlton can reach you?'

'That's not necessary. Before I leave, I was

hoping to catch up with some old friends. Hans Muller?'

She laughed. 'The big German guy with a terminal smoking habit? He comes in now and then. Was here just an hour or so ago. Talked to Chris about something.'

'Sorry I missed him. Blaine Dorsey?'

'Who?'

'Nothing. Well, thanks so much for your time. You've been very gracious. I like your sculpture.'

'Thanks. It's all for sale.'

'I'll be back.'

I opened the taxi's door, waking Mayer. He shook himself and smiled. 'Dozed off,' he said.

'Good. A nap is always nice. Do you think we could park somewhere where we wouldn't be seen by anyone in this building, but from where we could keep an eye on it?'

His face mirrored his puzzlement.

I said kindly, 'Nothing nefarious, Mr. Mayer. I'm just hoping to catch a glimpse of someone who I'd rather not see me.'

'I guess I could arrange that. Let's see.' He surveyed the area. 'How about over there? By the dock.'

'Looks good to me.'

We parked where he'd indicated. A few minutes later, I noticed his head drooping. 'Go ahead, Mr. Mayer, fall asleep. I'll let you know when it's time to leave.'

That time came a half hour later when Chris Turi pulled up in front of the studio, got out, and entered, followed by none other than Blaine Dorsey, Miki Dorsey's father. The car was familiar to me: Anne Harris's car, the one Turi had used to drive me to his house, and in which Anne had driven me back to Scott's Inn.

'Wake up, Mr. Mayer.'

I debated returning to the studio to see what another visit might result in. No, I decided. Another time. Besides, it was getting late, and I'd promised to be in touch with Vaughan Buckley regarding dinner that night.

But as we approached the inn, I asked Mayer to stop in front of Maurice St. James's gallery. It was a whim, pure and simple, but I had to do it.

I went inside, the tiny bell announcing my arrival. St. James was behind the counter. He looked up, smiled, and approached. 'Ah, Mrs. Fletcher. A pleasant surprise, twice in one day.'

'Twice?'

'We're having dinner together this evening. With the Buckleys.'

'I wasn't aware of that,' I said. 'But now that I am, I look doubly forward to it.'

'May I do something for you?'

'Perhaps. But only if you can keep a confidence.'

He leered conspiratorially. 'My middle name is discretion, Mrs. Fletcher.'

'That's good to hear. I might be interested in doing what I said the first time I was here.'

'Which was?'

'To buy a large number of Joshua Leopold paintings from you.'

His eyes widened, and he rubbed his hands together. 'An excellent decision, Mrs. Fletcher. Leopold's worth rises with each day. Any in particular?'

'No. I'll need time to carefully examine the lot, and I don't have that time now. Perhaps tomorrow.'

'Of course. I assure you I will offer you a very attractive price for them.'

'I would certainly expect that. In the meantime, not a word to anyone. Certainly, not to the Buckleys at dinner.'

He pressed his index finger to his lips. 'They are sealed, Mrs. Fletcher. Rest assured.'

CHAPTER NINETEEN

I knew one thing for certain. If Vaughan and Olga kept taking me to fancy restaurants for dinner, I was in for a month of serious dieting and exercise when I got home.

This night found us in a place called Nick and Toni's, a comfortable spot with an eclectic clientele. There were senior citizens, young families and babies, and a smattering of recognizable celebrities, including the singer Billy Joel (I didn't recognize him because I didn't know what he looked like, but Olga did the honors), New York Senator ·Alfonse D'Amato and a stunning woman I'd seen him with on C-SPAN, and who looked as though she'd be at home in Washington's power corridors, and later, the wonderful actress and author Shirley MacLaine, to whom I was introduced at the end of the evening.

Besides Vaughan, Olga, Maurice St. James, and me, the table included the couple I'd dined with my first night in the Hamptons, Jacob and Alix Simmons, both artist representatives from Manhattan, and a vivacious young travel writer, Laurie Wilson, who said she was in the Hamptons doing a magazine piece, and who might write a book for Buckley House on how the rich and famous vacation.

I admitted only to myself that I was not in an especially good mood. Jo Ann Forbes's murder had occurred less than twenty-four hours ago. The spirited, free-flowing conversation seemed out of place, although I didn't indicate my feelings about that. At least I wasn't at dinner with Hans Muller. That would have been too much to bear.

Funny, I thought, how we're able to shift mental gears over a period of time. As the evening wore on, I found myself thinking less about Jo Ann Forbes and more about the blatherskite at the table. Maybe it was the food; it flowed freely, too, beginning with thickly sliced Tuscan bread with Monini olive oil for dipping, huge fresh green salads, deep-fried zucchini chips, and then, at Vaughan's suggestion, grilled free-range chicken rubbed with rosemary and roasted garlic, and flash-cooked in an oven Vaughan claimed got up to over six hundred degrees. I love chicken, and pride myself on being a pretty good cook. But because I don't possess an oven capable of generating such intense heat, I could never duplicate the crisp skin that crackled and the incredibly juicy meat. The meal was topped off with a dessert of almond *biscotti* and Tuscan *vin santo*. Oh, my, I thought, daring to touch my waistline. How can people do this every night and not end up terminally obese?

My involuntary pushing of Jo Ann Forbes and her death from my mind was interrupted when Olga brought up the subject over second cups of coffee. 'How are you holding up, Jess?' she asked. 'Seeing that reporter's body this morning must have been dreadful.'

I nodded. 'It was, Olga. Not my idea of the way to start a day.'

'I hesitated mentioning that,' said St. James. 'Poor woman. Is there anything new on who might have done such a thing?'

'Not that I've heard,' I said. 'You?'

He shook his head. I asked the others. Negatives all around.

'I know one person who's sweating even bigger bullets than he usually does,' Vaughan

184

said.

'Hans,' Olga said.

'You bet,' said Vaughan. 'And I'm not feeling at all sorry for him. He called twice this afternoon. Wanted my help in dealing with the police, get his passport back. Some nerve. He claims to have lost our painting, then wants our help.'

'What painting?' St. James asked.

Vaughan explained.

'Hans didn't say anything to me about—'

Vaughan asked, 'Why would he have?'

St. James's smile was thin and forced. He waved his hand and said, 'Oh, for no reason. I just thought—'

'Did you see Mr. Muller today?' I asked the gallery owner.

'No.'

I waited a moment, then said, 'You're obviously a good friend of Blaine Dorsey.'

St. James replied, 'I know him. Not well. Frankly, I find the man to be distasteful, unpleasant.'

'Oh?'

'A most dishonest man. A scoundrel.'

'The dead model's father?' Vaughan said.

'Yes,' I said. 'He flew in from London, where he's involved in some capacity in the art world. From what I hear, his reputation there is less than savory. He's suspected of dealing in stolen art, and was a suspect in the murder of an artist not too long ago.'

185

As I spoke, I kept my eye on Maurice St. James, who appeared to become more uncomfortable with each word. When I'd finished laying out what I'd learned about Dorsey from my Scotland Yard friend, George Sutherland, I stared at St. James, awaiting a reaction.

'You seem to know a great deal about him,' was his comment.

'I've made a point of it.'

Vaughan looked at me, his smile saying, *What are you up to now?*

'You knew none of this, Maurice?' I asked the increasingly nervous gallery owner.

'No. It is all news to me, and unpleasant news at that. It is people like Dorsey who give those of us in the art world with integrity and honor a bad name. Don't you agree, Vaughan? Olga?'

They did.

'And Hans Muller,' St. James added. 'Oh, I suppose he's harmless enough—unless you are in a closed room with him and his dreaded cigarettes—' He laughed. 'But the circumstances of the poor young woman's death. Hans with her at a dinner party. Hours later, she is dead in his bedroom. And you say, Vaughan, he claims to have lost a painting belonging to you. I assume it was a valuable work.'

'Hard to say, Maurice. We were hoping to nail down its provenance. Hans said he'd help do that. That's why I let him take it last night.'

Maurice slowly shook his head and sighed loudly. 'It is all so unfortunate,' he said. 'Ah, well. Who can explain the behavior of some? Shall we end this lovely evening with brandy. Or perhaps a good port?'

We all declined.

Laurie Wilson, the travel writer, laughed as she said, 'Maybe I should think about writing a murder mystery set in the Hamptons instead of a travel guide.'

'Not a bad idea,' Vaughan said.

'I must go,' St. James said, standing, clicking his heels together and bowing slightly. 'This has been a splendid gathering, as expected. Mrs. Fletcher—Jessica—will I have the pleasure of seeing you again before you leave the Hamptons?'

'I'm sure you will.' Please don't kiss my hand, I thought. He seemed poised to do just that.

Shortly after St. James's departure, Ms. Wilson's sister, Pamela, arrived to pick her up.

'The night is young for you two, I assume,' said Vaughan after we'd been introduced.

The sisters laughed. 'Just a party,' Laurie Wilson said. 'This has been great, Vaughan. Thanks so much.'

'Give the book idea some more thought,' the publisher said.

As we watched the sisters leave, Vaughan announced, 'I think it's time for us to call it a

187

night, too. I have early tee off tomorrow at the club.'

His defection put a definitive end to the dinner. Vaughan introduced me to Shirley MacLaine, who was as gracious as I expected her to be, and we all went out to our cars. I expected to be driven back to the inn by my publisher and his wife. Instead, Vaughan headed in the direction of their house.

'Where are we going?' I asked.

'Home,' he replied. 'For that brandy or port. And a few questions for my favorite mystery writer.'

*   *   *

'. . . And so I went through her files,' I said, a brandy shimmering in an oversize snifter in my hand. 'That's when I found it. Most of Jo Ann's notes are in shorthand, but I think I made sense out of them.'

'And you're going to get together with the police chief tomorrow.'

'Yes. He has a set of the notes, too. What intrigues me is that Joshua Leopold and Miki Dorsey were lovers.'

'She was an active young lady,' said Olga, passing a plate of cheeses. 'Sexually, that is. You say she was intimately involved with this Chris Turi and with your instructor, Carlton Wells.'

'That's right. There's a set of notes from the

file that I am having trouble sorting out. My interpretation is that somehow Miki Dorsey lost her position with Leopold.'

'Her position?' Vaughan asked.

'A business arrangement with the artist. Besides being lovers, it seems that Miki functioned as Leopold's representative. At least early on. And it seems—again, I'm having trouble nailing down the literal meaning—it seems that Miki might have lost her status as his rep to Maurice St. James.'

Vaughan and Olga sat forward in their chairs. 'Maurice?' said Olga. 'How would he have stolen Leopold away from her?'

Vaughan answered. 'Money! Money fuels the art world, like it does just about everything else. Does that gibe with your notes, Jess?'

'Could be,' I said, sipping my brandy. It went down hot. 'What do you make of Maurice's derogatory comments at dinner about Miki Dorsey's father, Blaine Dorsey?'

'I don't know the man,' Vaughan said. 'Do you?'

'I've bumped into him a few times, and my friend with Scotland Yard, George Sutherland, gave me background on him.'

'So you mentioned at dinner,' Olga said. 'More brandy?'

'Heavens, no. From what I can piece together from Jo Ann's notes, Miki Dorsey started representing Joshua Leopold through her father in London. But then, if I'm correct,

189

Maurice St. James stole Leopold away from her. Blaine Dorsey was angry with Maurice when I overheard a conversation between them. Oh, by the way, I stopped in this afternoon at the studio where Joshua Leopold died. It's now a studio for Chris Turi and Carlton Wells.'

Vaughan shook his head. 'You've been busy, Jess.'

'I suppose I have. Vaughan, I've been contemplating doing something that might bring this to a head. If I decide to go ahead, I might need your help.'

'You know I'll do anything I can to help you, Jess. What is it that you're thinking of doing?'

'I need to give it more thought, Vaughan. In the meantime, I'm ready for bed. Call me a cab?'

'Where's your driver?'

'Fred Mayer? I sent him home. He'll pick me up at the inn in the morning.'

A half hour later I was in my room, in my robe and pajamas, and thinking back over this most traumatic of days. The sheer thought of it magnified my natural fatigue tenfold.

I went to the window and looked out. A fog had settled over the Hamptons, shrouding the garden's trees and shrubs in wispy, swirling cotton as the breeze propelled it.

As I was about to turn away from the window and give in to my weariness, a momentary flicker of orange light caught my eye. I leaned closer to the window, placed my nose against it, and squinted. There it was again. My initial thought was of World War II, when blackout drills were routine. A cigarette can be seen from an aircraft, we were warned.

Or seen through the fog from a window.

The light glowed again, then fell to the ground, and a shadow moved through the fog, away from the tree behind which it had been, and out the rear gate.

I drew the drapes tight across the window and climbed into bed. Should I call downstairs and ask Mr. Scott to go outside to check on what I'd seen? That wouldn't be fair to him.

Call the police? Call 911?

And tell them what? That someone was trespassing?

It wasn't my property.

As I allowed sleep to overcome me, I made a decision. I was close to having had enough of the Hamptons, enough of art and artists, of art dealers and gallery owners—of all of it.

I'd give it another few days. Whether I got to the bottom of things or not, I'd pack my bags and head home to Cabot Cove, where things were . . . well, where things were *normal*.

The contemplation made me smile as my eyes closed and I drifted off.

CHAPTER TWENTY

'I suppose you're right, Mrs. Fletcher. But I'm not sure I see how these things link up.'

Police Chief Cramer and I had gone over every word on the three pages taken from Jo Ann Forbes's file marked LEOPOLD, JOSHUA. Some entries were complete enough to make obvious sense to both of us. Others were subject to interpretation, and our interpretations often differed.

'Let me see if I understand your thesis, Mrs. Fletcher,' Cramer said. 'You're saying that because of the dead artist, Leopold, these other things have happened—Ms. Dorsey's death and the murder of the reporter, Jo Ann Forbes.'

'That's right. Interesting, you continue to differentiate between Miki Dorsey's "death," and Jo Ann Forbes's "murder." '

His eyebrows went up. 'And you feel *both* were murder.'

'I feel that there's a good possibility that Miki Dorsey's death was not by natural causes. Would you, *could* you arrange for a second autopsy on her?'

He slowly spun in his chair so that he faced away from me. I heard him sigh deeply. Obviously, my request was one with which he'd just as soon not deal.

He completed his 360-degree spin and again looked at me. 'That's easier said than done, Mrs. Fletcher. Her father has been badgering us to release his daughter's body so he can take her back to London. Frankly, I don't have much to stand on to keep her here.'

'Except that, as you told me, you share my feelings that she might have been killed. As I recall, you said there were certain people reinforcing that view for you. Who are they?'

'I can't tell you. But I will say that they include an individual who is—well, let me just say that he's not without some influence.'

I didn't press for him to break his trust. It wouldn't have done any good even if I had. Chief Cramer was obviously a man of integrity and honor. But at least I knew that this unnamed individual was a man.

But I decided to again raise the issue of having a second autopsy performed on Miki Dorsey. Cramer's reaction when I originally brought it up wasn't a flat turndown. All he'd said was that it wouldn't be easy.

'Can you?' I said. 'Arrange for a second autopsy on Miki Dorsey?'

'I can try.'

'But *will* you?'

His expression was thoughtful. 'Yes,' he said. 'I'll pull out all the stops.'

'Thank you.'

'No, thank *you*, Mrs. Fletcher. Ordinarily, I'd be annoyed with a civilian injecting herself into what is my area of responsibility. But in your case—'

'Yes?'

'In your case I think you'll be more of a help than a hindrance. You've already proved that. I'll push for the second autopsy.'

'Good. Now, in regard to that, I would like to have the opportunity to speak with the coroner before that second autopsy is performed.'

'Why?'

'To share with him some knowledge that could be useful.'

'Which is?'

I would have preferred not to reveal what George Sutherland told me about the powerful poison, ricin. But I felt I owed it to this very nice chief of police. I outlined for him what ricin was, how it worked, and how it could easily escape detection during an autopsy unless the examiner was specifically looking for such a lethal substance. Cramer listened attentively.

When I finished, he grunted and stood behind his desk. 'You're a remarkable woman, Mrs. Fletcher. I'm impressed.'

'Thank you for the compliment, but please don't be impressed. All I want is to get to the bottom of these tragic events and return to my home in Maine.'

'Then, let's work together to see that you get back home as quickly as possible.'

As he walked me to the front door of police headquarters, I asked when Jo Ann Forbes's autopsy would be completed.

'It was an hour ago,' he said. 'The blow to the head did it.'

'Any leads?'

'Muller.'

'Are you charging him with her murder?'

'Between us?'

'Of course.'

'Probably. But not today. The DA feels there's enough circumstantial evidence to indict, and wants to go forward. I've persuaded him to allow us to develop whatever additional evidence might be out there to strengthen the case. ' In the meantime, Mr. Muller is threatening everything from suing us to a nuclear response by Germany.'

I couldn't help but smile. 'He does tend to be dramatic,' I said.

'If only he didn't smoke so much. The interrogation room became uninhabitable.'

'Well, thanks for everything this morning. We'll keep in touch. Can I talk to the coroner?'

'I'll set something up.'

Fred Mayer was waiting. When he picked me up earlier that morning at Scott's Inn, I detected the smell of alcohol in the cab. His eyes were watery, and he hadn't shaved. I asked if he was feeling okay.

'Tip-top, Mrs. Fletcher. You?'

'Fine.' I somehow didn't believe him, but wasn't about to mount a challenge. It was possible I'd been tainted by Chief Cramer's comment about my driver, that he was perhaps too fond of 'the grape,' as the saying goes. I decided that unless he drank while in my employ, I had no right to question what he did when he wasn't on duty. And so I said nothing else.

I had Mayer drive me to the house shared by Miki Dorsey, Chris Turi, and others. It was a lovely day by the water, sunny and bright, a light onshore breeze bringing that invigorating tangy salt smell to my nostrils. We parked in the driveway, and I sat quietly in the rear seat. Eventually, Mayer asked what I intended to do.

'Go inside,' I replied, 'after I put a few things in mental order.' I finally got out, went to the front door, and was about to knock when it opened.

'Ms. Peckham,' I said. 'Jessica Fletcher.'

'I don't forget people that easily,' she said.

Waldine Peckham was the older member of the household, the artist who'd been painting during my first visit. By 'older,' I mean only slightly older. I judged her to be in her thirties. There was a no-nonsense quality about her that I liked and to which I related. She was obviously not a woman to be trifled with, nor would she suffer fools easily. All points in her favor.

'Here to see the grieving boyfriend?' she asked, one hand on a cocked hip.

'Chris? No. I actually came to see you.'

'Why?' No beating around the bush with her.

'May I come in and explain?'

'Sure. I was on my way out, but it's nothing important.'

We went to the living room. I was pleased to see that no one else was there. Waldine walked to an easel holding a painting on which she was working: a still life of a bowl of flowers on a nearby table.

'That's very nice,' I said.

'Not bad. I'll ruin it.'

'Why do you say that?'

'I ruin everything I paint. But that's not why you're here.'

'No, it's not. Can we sit?'

We sat on a well-worn couch. Waldine, who wore tight jeans, a yellow sweatshirt, and tan cowboy boots, propped the boots on the edge of a scarred coffee table. She turned to look at me; her expression said, *Go ahead. I'm listening.*

'I was wondering whether you'd be interested in joining me in some playacting.'

'Playacting? I'm an artist, not an actress. Actually, I'm not much of an artist, either. Playact?' She laughed; it was a pleasant, guttural laugh that did wonders to lighten her

197

persona.

'I don't mean you'd have to act exactly, Waldine.'

'It's Wally. My friends call me Wally.'

'You won't have to be an actress, Wally. All you'd have to do is pretend that you're interested in buying a certain work of art.'

'Oh? What work of art?'

It was my turn to laugh.

'I'm afraid I overstated it,' I said. 'Are you aware that a sketch I did in the class where Miki Dorsey died was stolen from me?'

'I read about it.'

'And that it was stolen again from *Dan's Papers*?'

'That, too. Is that what you expect me to pretend I want to buy?'

'Yes.'

'How much is it worth?'

'To me, nothing. To someone else? Who knows? I understand the asking price is up to three thousand dollars.'

She directed a stream of air through her lips. 'That's a lot of money.'

'I wouldn't expect you to pay, Wally. I'll advance the money for you to use.'

She got up and paced in front of the couch. 'Why me?'

'No special reason, except I like and trust you. It would be important that this remain a secret between us, at least until you've successfully gotten the sketch back for me.'

She stopped pacing. 'How do I do this?' she asked.

'Let me lay it out for you, Wally.'

*   *   *

Once Wally Peckham agreed to help, I left the house and told Fred Mayer I was ready for lunch. He dropped me at a roadside fish restaurant that appeared to be barely more than a shack. It turned out that the Lobster Roll Restaurant was a lot more than its physical plant suggested. I downed a superb lobster roll and coffee, and even opted for dessert, heated raspberry pie with cinnamon ice cream. Somehow, having met with Chief Cramer and putting my idea into play with Wally Peckham had lifted a feeling of heaviness I'd been experiencing. Psychotherapists often say that any action is better than no action. I think they're right.

Until that morning I'd been floundering. Things had happened at such a dizzying pace that I hadn't the time to sort through them. At times, it was a surrealistic experience—called to the scene of a young reporter's murder at four in the morning, then having dinner in a fancy restaurant that same night with friends.

I thought back to the day I left Manhattan on the Hampton Jitney for ten days of rest, relaxation, and quiet art lessons. That day, I'd been approached by a drug dealer, witnessed a senseless attack, and saw my books being illegally sold on the street. What had I thought as I climbed on the jitney? *I've had enough crime to last a good long time.*

And here I was, surrounded by physical beauty and lovely people, and all I'd experienced was stolen art—and murder.

I had to do something. I couldn't go back to Cabot Cove and spend the rest of my life wondering whether Miki Dorsey and Joshua Leopold had died natural deaths. And I certainly couldn't simply erase from my memory the sight of Jo Ann Forbes, whom I'd gotten to know a little, sprawled in Hans Muller's tiny bedroom.

I had to do something.

I'd invited Fred Mayer to join me for lunch, but he declined, opting instead for a hamburger from a fast-food outlet down the street.

'How was it?' he asked after we'd joined up again in his taxi.

'Wonderful. With any luck I'll taste the lobster roll for the rest of the day.'

He smiled and started the engine. 'Just want to satisfy my customer's needs, Mrs. Fletcher. Where are we going this afternoon?'

'First stop,' I said, 'is Scott's Inn. I need to check on my messages.'

'We can call,' he offered.

'No, I'd rather go back. There are a few other things I need to do there.'

200

Joe Scott was at his small desk when I entered the inn. He greeted me warmly, and asked if there was anything he could do for me.

'As a matter of fact, there is. Would it be possible to arrange with the phone company to run a private line into my room?'

He pondered the question for a moment before replying, 'I have a second line into the inn. Would it suffice to have an extension of that number installed for you?'

It was my turn to consider. 'I suppose so,' I said, 'but a totally new line and number would really work better. Naturally, I'll pay any costs involved.'

'Then, it's a new line and number you'll have. My brother-in-law works for the phone company. I assume you want it now.'

'Isn't that always the case?' I said, smiling and sighing.

'Not to worry, Mrs. Fletcher. I'll take care of it right away.'

'Thank you. Any calls for me?'

He handed me a batch of pink message slips. I ruffled through them.

Two calls were from Cabot Cove: Dr. Seth Hazlitt, and Sheriff Morton Metzger. Call them back.

Vaughan Buckley left a message that he'd be out until three, but wanted me to call him at home after that.

Maurice St. James said that he expected me

201

to stop by his gallery that day.

A reporter from *Dan's Papers*, Rich Norris, asked for an interview regarding the murder of Jo Ann Forbes.

And Police Chief Cramer—funny, I thought, but I never did learn his first name—asked me to contact him at my earliest convenience.

Because it was only two o'clock, it was too early to return Vaughan's call. But I did want to see what was on Chief Cramer's mind. I went to my room and called headquarters.

'You said you wanted a chance to speak with Dr. Eder, the Suffolk County coroner,' he said.

My heart tripped. Did that mean Cramer had been successful in calling for a second autopsy on Miki Dorsey?

'That's right,' I said.

'Here's his number, Mrs. Fletcher. He said he'd be happy to meet with you.'

'That's wonderful, Chief. By the way, do you have a first name?'

'Afraid I do.'

'Oh?'

'Hopeful.'

'Hopeful? That's your name?'

'Yup. My friends call me Hope. You can imagine the confusion that causes.'

'I take it your parents were optimists.'

'They certainly were. Well, you know my secret now.'

'I think it's a perfectly fine name, but I'll call you Chief Cramer.'

He laughed. 'A diplomat through and through.'

'Any luck in arranging a second autopsy on Ms. Dorsey?' I asked.

'As a matter of fact, yes. I think the district attorney is leaning my way. I should know by the end of the day.'

'I *hope* he—'

We both laughed, and I promised to check in later.

I called the number given me by Chief Cramer for Dr. Peter Eder. After going through a series of voicemail selections—how annoying they are—Dr. Eder came on the line. 'Chief Cramer said you'd be calling,' he said. 'It's a pleasure speaking with you, Mrs. Fletcher. My wife is a true fan, has read most of your books.'

'That's always pleasant to hear, Dr. Eder. Did Chief Cramer tell you what it was I wished to discuss?'

'No. But he did say I'd find it fascinating. In what is a basically dull existence, the thought of something fascinating is always appealing.'

'When can we meet?'

'The end of today? I plan to be in the Hamptons this evening.'

'That would be fine. Where and when?'

'I have a satellite office there. Say, six?'

'Fine.' He gave me the address, and we concluded the conversation.

I freshened up, and was about to go

downstairs when the innkeeper, Joe Scott, knocked. 'Just wanted you to know, Mrs. Fletcher, that they'll be installing the line into this room within the hour.'

'Splendid. I hope you know how appreciative I am, Mr. Scott.'

'I have no doubt about that, Mrs. Fletcher. You're the sort of person who appreciates things. I knew that the minute I met you.'

'I'm flattered.'

'And pretty soon you'll have a phone of your own. Oh, by the way, you've already got your number.' He gave it to me on a slip of paper. 'Just one request,' he said.

'What's that?'

'Keep it quiet. I don't want other guests asking for the same thing.'

'Our secret is safe with me. Thanks again.'

I had Fred Mayer stop at a public phone where I called Waldine Peckham at the group house. 'I have a number for you,' I said. She wrote it down. I quickly went over the plan I'd presented her at the house. As I was finishing up, I heard what I thought sounded like a receiver being lowered into its cradle.

'Wally, is there someone else on the line?' I asked.

'I don't think so. The only other person here is Anne.'

'Well, I guess you can get started.'

'I don't know why I'm doing this,' she said, laughing.

'Call it a thirst for adventure.'

'You can call it that,' she said. 'I'll let you know if I hear anything. 'Bye.'

So much for that.

Next stop, Maurice St. James's gallery.

CHAPTER TWENTY-ONE

The tiny bell tinkled as I entered St. James's gallery, where a young couple in Bermuda shorts, and with an infant in a stroller, took in the works of Joshua Leopold. A girl still in her teens cleaned glass on the paintings with Windex and paper towels. She looked at me, said nothing, and continued to wipe.

I approached her. 'Is Mr. St. James in?' I asked.

Without missing a beat with her chore, she replied, 'He's in the back.'

'Would you please get him for me?'

My interference into her routine was obviously the source of great annoyance. She sighed, pouted, placed the roll of paper towels on a table, and disappeared through the door.

'He wants to know who wants to see him,' she said when she returned.

'Mrs. Fletcher. Jessica Fletcher.'

She disappeared again. A moment later St. James emerged, a broad smile on his face. 'Ah, Mrs. Fletcher, I knew I'd see you today. What a pleasure.'

'I received your message and thought I'd stop in.'

'Delighted. Delighted.'

He took my elbow and guided me to a far corner, stopping to wish the departing young couple a pleasant vacation. 'Always browsers, never buyers,' he muttered. His face brightened. 'But there are exceptions, aren't there, Mrs. Fletcher?'

'Obviously. How is Joshua Leopold selling these days?'

'Fine. Slow. A transition period.'

'How so?'

'Artists on the ascendancy always suffer peaks and valleys. Like the stock market. Are you an investor?'

'A modest one. Very conservative.'

'Certificates of deposit.'

'And a stock or two. Mr. St. James, could we go someplace where we can talk? Privately?'

'Unfortunately, here in the gallery is probably the most private place I can think of.'

I found his comment interesting. Until then I'd assumed he was well-to-do, and that his gallery was prospering. That evidently wasn't true.

'All right,' I said. 'When I first came into the gallery, I jokingly said I was interested in buying every painting here. Remember?'

'Of course, Mrs. Fletcher. But I didn't take it as a joke.'

'I gathered that, which is why I clarified myself the next time we met. But maybe it wasn't as much of a joke as originally intended.'

'I'm listening.'

'I might be interested in buying a number of Joshua Leopold's paintings from you. Not everything, of course. But selected pieces.'

'I think that represents a prudent approach to collecting art,' he said. 'Choose those works that represent the artist at his best, that have the greatest potential for appreciation.'

'Exactly. My financial adviser in Maine has been urging me to diversify my investments. He is a strong believer in collectibles, which, of course, includes art.'

'You have an astute adviser, Mrs. Fletcher. The potential value of paintings certainly runs far ahead of the stock market, real estate, or any other more mundane investment strategy.'

'That's precisely what he said, Mr. St. James.'

'Maurice.'

'Maurice, let me be perfectly candid with you. Some of Leopold's works on these walls are quite good. But they represent what I consider to be—well, they are pedestrian, if only because they are on public display, available to anyone who happens to wander into this gallery.'

'Mrs. Fletcher, I—I see your point. Of course. Besides being a best-selling writer of books, you are a businesswoman.'

'Thank you. Now, let's take this conversation to a second level.'

'Yes. Absolutely. Would you like to go to my office? A place to sit? Tea? Something stronger?'

'That would be appreciated.'

His office was small and cluttered with antique furniture. There were wooden file cabinets, a computer, and piles of oversize books, all having to do with art. St. James removed some of the books from an armchair and pulled it up to his desk for me. He sat behind the desk, leaned forward, and rested his chin on a shelf formed with his long, slender fingers. 'Tea?' he asked. 'I'll have the young woman make some.'

'No, thank you,' I replied, not wanting to further distract her from her glass-cleaning obligations. 'Perhaps I'd better get to the point, Maurice.'

'If you wish.'

'I would like to buy some of Joshua Leopold's less well-known works. Works that are in the hands of private collectors.'

He leaned back, his fingers still beneath his chin. 'Private collectors,' he repeated softly. 'That isn't easy, Mrs. Fletcher.'

'I don't expect it is. And call me Jessica.'

'Of course. Don't misunderstand. There are a number of Joshua's finer works in private hands. After all, that's what successful collectors do, cull the best from an artist's output.'

'Exactly,' I said. 'I want to buy Joshua Leopold's best work.'

'Well, Jessica, what I have to offer in this gallery represents some of his finer efforts.'

I shook my head. 'I think you know what I mean,' I said, injecting a modicum of gravity into my voice.

He raised his chin and closed his eyes, as if in deep thought. Then, he opened his eyes, leaned forward, and said, 'I know precisely what you mean, Jessica. And I think I can he of immeasurable help to you.'

'I never doubted that for a moment, Maurice.'

'But I must be candid, Jessica. Gaining access to such works carries with it a certain— well, let me just say there is a certain risk involved.'

'Risk? Tell me about it.'

'The wrong word, perhaps. "Discretion" might be more accurate. Some of these works have ended up in private hands through unconventional channels. Do you follow me?'

' "Unconventional channels," ' I repeated. 'Stolen? Misrouted?'

'I like that, Jessica. Misrouted. Yes, that sums it up, I think.'

'I have no problem with that. When can I see some pieces? I don't plan to stay in the Hamptons much longer.'

'Then, time is of the essence.'

'Yes it is.'

'I need twenty-four hours.'

'That's reasonable,' I said, standing and straightening my skirt. 'Shall I call you then?'

'Better that I call you. I have the Scott's Inn number.'

'Let me give you another number, Maurice.' I wrote out for him the number of the new phone in my room.

I climbed back into Fred Mayer's taxi.

'Next?' he asked.

'A store where I can buy a telephone answering machine.'

CHAPTER TWENTY-TWO

Dr. Peter Eder's Hamptons office was located in a small community hospital. As he warmly welcomed me, I realized he was not as old as he appeared from the steps of town hall. His smile was wide and genuine, his overall demeanor pleasant and outgoing, a personality one seldom expects from a coroner.

It was a spare and Spartan office, with standard-issue metal furniture and an assortment of medical equipment hanging on the walls. The Suffolk County coroner wore a white lab coat over a blue shirt and red tie. Half glasses were tethered by a red-and-white ribbon behind his neck. He'd been going through a *Yellow Pages* directory open on his desk.

'A pleasure meeting you,' he said, closing the directory. 'I have years of medical training but can't get my VCR programmed. I was looking for someone to do that. Please, have a seat. Chief Cramer says you have something important to discuss with me.'

'Yes, I do, Dr. Eder. It has to do with the autopsy you performed on Miki Dorsey.'

He nodded.

'I've asked Chief Cramer to try and arrange for a second autopsy on her.'

'He told me that.'

'Did he tell you why?'

'No. He said I'd have the pleasure of hearing it directly from you.'

'He's right. Miki Dorsey died in front of my eyes. And I'd become a friend of sorts with the reporter who was murdered, Jo Ann Forbes.'

'I didn't know that,' said Eder, his smile replaced with a frown. 'Very sad what happened to Ms. Forbes. It was a vicious blow that killed her. Someone very strong, I'd say.'

I immediately thought of Hans Muller. He certainly was big. But I suspected he wasn't what you'd call strong. Flabby was more like it, a body bloated with alcohol.

My attention snapped back to Dr. Eder. 'Doctor,' I said, 'I have reason to believe that Miki Dorsey did not die of a heart attack.'

211

'I'm aware of your reputation, Mrs. Fletcher, but I'm afraid I'm going to have to question the conclusion you've reached. My autopsy on Ms. Dorsey was thorough. She died as the result of a coronary thrombosis, leading to a myocardial infarction. Textbook case. No debate about it. Certainly, no doubt or reservation in my mind.'

I knew coming into his office that I had to avoid questioning his professional competence if I were to gain his cooperation. Actually, I wasn't doubting his credentials and skills. From what George Sutherland told me, it would take a medical examiner actively looking for something like ricin to find it. There was no reason for Dr. Eder to be searching for traces of this highly lethal drug, used primarily by clandestine operatives. Why would he? In the Hamptons? Hardly a place where murderous international spies would be acting out their deadly game.

'Dr. Eden I'm sure that every sign pointed to Miki Dorsey having died from natural causes. As you say, from coronary thrombosis that led to a—?'

'Myocardial infarction.'

'Yes. Myocardial infarction. Doctor, have you ever heard of a poisonous substance called ricin?'

He chewed his cheek as he searched his medical mind for the answer. 'No,' he said, 'I can't say that I have.'

I told him what George Sutherland had told me about ricin. He listened attentively. When I was through, he smiled and shook his head. 'I'm afraid my medical training and clinical experience have spared me from Cold War cops-and-robbers poisons. You're saying that it's possible that Ms. Dorsey was killed by someone, using this substance?'

'I'm saying that I don't know and would like to find out. Do you remember doing an autopsy on an artist who died here about a year ago? A young man named Joshua Leopold.'

'Of course I do. A few months after his death, I went out and bought one of his paintings. It hangs in my den.'

'That's nice. He was very young. Like Miki Dorsey.'

'I recall. Early thirties, I think.'

'A coronary thrombosis, leading to a—'

'Myocardial infarction.' We said it in unison.

'Him, too, Mrs. Fletcher?'

I nodded. 'Him, too.'

'You've got to give me something tangible.'

'Dr. Eder, I could go through all the scraps of disparate information I've collected. For me, those scraps add up to a good possibility that the deaths of Joshua Leopold, Miki Dorsey, and Jo Ann Forbes have a common thread running through them.'

'Ms. Forbes, too?'

'Yes.'

'And what is that thread, Mrs. Fletcher?'

'Art.'

'Joshua Leopold's art?'

'I think so. And since you now own a Leopold, I would think you'd want to know how the artist really died.'

'Uh-huh. Tell you what. If Hope Cramer and the DA agree, we'll do another autopsy on Ms. Dorsey. But only after I come up with the necessary information and technique to test for this ricin.'

'How quickly can you do that?'

'I'll get on it first thing in the morning. There's a forensic pathologist in the city I'll confer with. If he doesn't know, no one does.'

'I appreciate this very much, Doctor. One last request?'

'Shoot.'

'When you confer with this pathologist, could you arrange to have these tested for ricin?'

I took from my pocket the two cigarette butts I'd gathered up before leaving the inn that afternoon, one smoked by Miki Dorsey just before she died, the other found by the tree outside Scott's Inn. I also laid on the gray metal desktop the package of cigarettes I'd picked up from Chris Turi's area of the artist's studio he shared with Carlton Wells. I separated Miki Dorsey's last smoke from the other items. 'This is the cigarette I think might have delivered ricin to Miki Dorsey. This other

214

half-smoked butt might have come from this package, Doctor. I don't know whether any lab could ascertain that, but I'd appreciate it if you'd ask.'

'Of course I will. Anything else?'

'No.'

'I have a question for you,' he said.

I smiled. 'As you said, "shoot."'

'If you're correct, Mrs. Fletcher, who killed Ms. Dorsey? Who killed Ms. Forbes?'

'Let me add a name. Who killed Joshua Leopold?'

'Well?' he said, head cocked, eyes narrowed.

'As soon as I figure that out, you'll be among the first to know. Thanks again, Doctor. I hope you get your VCR programmed. A friend of mine back in Maine got mine working.'

The ringing phone on his desk interrupted. Eder picked up. 'Yes, Hope, she's right here, about to leave.' He handed the receiver to me. 'Chief Cramer.'

'Hello, Chief.'

'Hello, Mrs. Fletcher. Just thought you'd want to know that Mr. Hans Muller has disappeared.'

'Disappeared? I thought you pulled his passport.'

'We did. But that doesn't mean he can't travel anywhere in the United States. He was told not to leave the Hamptons. Looks to me like he's saying loud and clear that he's guilty.'

'Juries are told not to make such an

215

inference,' I said.

'That doesn't mean *I* infer it. I've put out an all-points on Muller. If you hear from him, tell him he's making a big mistake. Tell him to turn himself in. And call me.'

'I certainly will, Chief. Thanks for letting me know.'

CHAPTER TWENTY-THREE

A quick stop at Scott's Inn enabled me to attach my recently acquired answering machine to the phone that had been installed in my absence. I recorded a simple outgoing message, stating only that the caller had reached the assigned number and to leave a message following the beep.

Downstairs, I picked up the phone on Joe Scott's desk and called my new number. My message came through loud and clear. Good, I thought. It's working. My inability to hook up things electrical rivaled Dr. Eder's skill at programming his VCR.

I went back upstairs and used the new phone to call Vaughan Buckley.

'I was getting worried about you,' he said. 'Where have you been?'

'Out and about. Sorry to be so late in returning your call.'

'Somehow,' he said, 'your idyllic vacation in

the Hamptons hasn't turned out quite the way Olga and I envisioned it.'

'Best laid plans and all that,' I said. 'Am I interrupting dinner?'

'No. But we are getting ready to go out. We're hoping you'll join us.'

'Depends on who else will be there. Goodness, that sounds pompous, but I've had enough art talk to last a good long while.'

He laughed. 'They can be a bit much, can't they, artists and their followers. As a matter of fact, there isn't an artist or artist's rep or gallery owner on the horizon for this evening. Just Olga and me, and a few friends from publishing who have homes out here.'

'That was another subject I pledged to avoid. Writers and publishers, present company an exception, of course.'

'Of course. Still have that driver on call?'

'Mr. Mayer? Yes. He's downstairs waiting for me.'

'Tell him to go home. We'll pick you up.'

'No, I—it's too late for that. He's planned his evening around driving me. Just tell me where to meet you.'

'Everything okay with you, Jess?'

'Yes. Everything is fine.'

His silence said he wasn't buying it, but he didn't follow through, saying instead, 'Olga and our friends are in the mood for Mexican food. There's a good Tex-Mex restaurant, Santa Fe Junction. They don't take

217

reservations, but we won't have to wait long.'
He gave me the address.

Mexican food has never been high on my
list of favorite cuisines, with Indian food
rivaling it. 'That would be fine,' I said, thinking
I can always find something on the menu that
wouldn't go down too hot and hard. 'See you
at eight.'

I quickly freshened up and was about to
leave the suite when the ringing of a phone
stopped me in my tracks. I looked at the
instrument on the nightstand next to the bed,
then at the new phone sitting on the small
desk. It was the new one clamoring for my
attention.

I stood at the desk as it continued ringing.
As I was about to pick it up, my voice came
through the tiny speaker on the answering
machine, giving my outgoing message to
whoever was calling. When I was finished, the
familiar voice and German accent of Hans
Muller said: 'Mrs. Fletcher. It is Hans Muller.
Are you there?'

Why was he calling on a number that had
been installed only hours ago? Who had I
given the number to? Wally Peckham. Maurice
St. James. That was it.

'Mrs. Fletcher, please, if you are there pick
up the phone. I must speak with you.'

I drew a breath, exhaled, and slowly moved
my hand toward the receiver.

'Mrs. Fletcher, I know I offended you when

218

we last spoke. I apologize. I throw myself at your feet. Please, if you are there I—'

'Mr. Muller?' I said into the mouthpiece.

He sounded like a large balloon deflating. 'Ah, Mrs. Fletcher. You are there. Thank goodness.'

'Mr. Muller, are you aware the police are looking for you. They've put out an all-points bulletin.'

'*Ya*. I know.'

'Where are you? Why have you chosen to disappear?'

Another lengthy, heavy sigh. 'Because—because, I have not done what they say I have done. I did not kill Ms. Forbes. You believe that, don't you?'

'What I believe doesn't matter. The important thing is that you turn yourself in to the police immediately. If you're innocent, you'll have the chance to prove that in the proper way and under the proper circumstances. Running away will only hurt you, not help.'

There was silence.

'Mr. Muller. Are you there?'

'*Ya*, I am here, Mrs. Fletcher. And you are right, good lady. But I must speak with you before I make such a decision.'

'Where are you, Mr. Muller?'

'You will come?'

'No. But where are you?'

'I will not say unless you promise to come to

219

me.'

'Mr. Muller, I'm on my way to dinner with friends, and I—'

'The Buckleys?'

'Yes, as a matter of fact. How did you get this number? It's new.'

'A friend.'

'Maurice St. James? He knows where you are?'

'I must go.'

'Mr. Muller, please. Listen to me. If you agree to turn yourself in, I'll pave the way with the police. I know Chief Cramer. I'll talk to him. I promise I'll—'

The click of the phone being lowered into its cradle jarred my ear.

I pondered my next move. There was a good chance that Muller had called from Maurice St. James's gallery. I had to assume it was St. James who'd given Muller my new number.

But I hesitated running downstairs, jumping into Fred Mayer's taxi, and going to the gallery to confirm my suspicion. It wasn't my place to assume the responsibility of a bounty hunter, tracking down a possible murderer.

I called police headquarters. Naturally, I didn't expect Chief Hopeful Cramer to be there at that hour, but I was wrong. He'd stayed late to catch up on paperwork.

'Sorry to bother you at night, Chief, but I thought it was important,'

'What is it, Mrs. Fletcher?'

'I just received a call from Hans Muller.'

'Really? Where is he?'

'He didn't say. But he wanted me to come to him. I declined.'

'That was prudent. No idea where he is?'

'Only one possibility. The art gallery downtown owned by Maurice St. James.'

'I know it. Why do you think Muller might be there?'

'Just because—well, just chalk it up to intuition.'

'That's good enough for me. I'll have a car over there in minutes.'

'Good. Will you be at headquarters long enough to know whether they picked up Muller?'

'I'll make a point of it.'

'I'll call. A half hour?'

'That should give us enough time.'

The minute I hung up, I knew I couldn't just sit in the room for thirty minutes. I got into Mayer's cab and told him to drive by St. James's gallery, but to keep a distance. When we arrived, I saw two uniformed officers knocking on the gallery's front door. One went to the back, but reappeared only a minute later. They looked at each other, shrugged, got back in their patrol car and took off. Obviously, no one was there. Or, if Muller *was* inside, he was laying low in the shadows.

Although I already knew Chief Cramer's officers hadn't found Hans Muller at the gallery, I made my promised call from a booth.

'No one there,' Cramer said. 'I considered trying to get hold of the gallery owner, St. James, but the investigating officers are convinced no one was inside.'

'I'm sure they're right. Well, Chief Cramer, if I hear from him again, I'll call immediately.'

'Thanks for your help, Mrs. Fletcher. By the way, the coroner was impressed with your presentation to him.'

'That's nice to hear, and it's thanks to you. I'm off to dinner with friends at Santa Fe Junction, but I'll keep in touch.'

'My favorite Tex-Mex restaurant out here, Mrs. Fletcher. Enjoy!'

When I told Fred Mayer where I was going, he asked, 'You like that kind of food?'

'Not especially.'

'Maybe you'd better take these with you.' He reached into his shirt pocket and handed me a half-eaten roll of Tums.

I laughed. 'Really think it will be that bad?' I asked.

'Even worse. Good luck.'

I was the last one to join the dinner party, which had already been seated in a large green Naugahyde banquette with a maroon tablecloth. A cactus plant sat in the middle of the table. I was introduced to the others by Vaughan, and took the last available seat in the crowded booth. Everyone had been served their drinks; I opted for sparkling water with

222

plenty of ice (getting ready for the hot stuff), and a wedge of lime.

A minute after I'd been served, the waitress returned with an appetizer Vaughan had ordered for the table. I'd never seen anything quite like it, and asked what it was called.

'Onion Blossom,' the pretty and pert waitress said as she served it to us.

'You'll love it,' Olga said. 'They take a whole onion and peel it, then cut off the top and bottom, slice it into wedges and dip it in tempura batter. A little cilantro and chili pepper, and then into the deep fryer.'

We each had our own Onion Blossom. I stared at the one in front of me. It had opened into a crispy flower during deep-frying. It was beautiful.

'Dip it in the avocado sauce,' Vaughan said.

It was as delicious as it was visually attractive. If the rest of the meal was as good, I might change my view of Southwestern cooking.

We'd just been served our main courses when the young man who'd greeted me at the door came to the table. 'Mrs. Fletcher?' he said.

I looked up from my hot plate of mesquite-grilled vegetables and penne. 'Yes?'

'There's a phone call for you.'

'For me? Who can it be?'

I excused myself and went to the manager's podium, where a phone was off the hook. I picked it up and said, 'Hello?'

'Mrs. Fletcher, Chief Cramer here. Sorry to disturb your dinner.'

'That's quite all right. I did tell you where I'd be. Is something wrong?'

'Maybe there's something right. We know where Muller is.'

'Wonderful.'

'He's holed up in a boathouse down near the town dock.'

'How did you find him?'

'A patrol officer saw this big guy duck into the boathouse. Checked it out. Says it's Muller.'

'Is the boathouse surrounded?'

'Yup. We're just sitting and waiting. We don't have a negotiating team like they do in the city, but we've been talking to him.'

'And?'

'Mr. Hans Muller says he won't come out unless he talks to you first.'

'Talks to *me*?'

'That's what he says.'

'That's preposterous. Can't you just go in and take him? He's not armed, is he?'

'Negative on that, Mrs. Fletcher. He's got a handgun. And he threatens to kill himself unless he gets to talk to you.'

'Oh, my.'

'That's what I say, only my choice of words is a little different. Look, Mrs. Fletcher, I need you. You can head off a nasty episode just by talking with him. I'm sending a car for you. Should be there any minute.'

'I have a taxi waiting outside. We'll follow.'

'Whatever you say. And thanks.'

I hung up and turned to face the booth where my dinner companions were talking and laughing. What would I tell them? That the food hadn't set well with me, and I needed to go home immediately? That I had a headache or a toothache?

I decided the only course of action was to tell them exactly why I was leaving.

My announcement caused sudden and total silence. It was Vaughan who broke it. 'I absolutely won't allow you to do this,' he said, covering my hand with his on the table. 'Hans sounds as though he's gone off the deep end. No telling what he might do to you. Hold you hostage. Even kill you. He might have killed Ms. Forbes. Nothing to lose by killing you.'

'I'll be with the police,' I said. 'They'll—'

'This is so exciting,' one of my dinner companions said.

'Can we go with you?' said another.

The door to the restaurant opened, and a uniformed patrolman came through. I stood and motioned for him. He came to the table.

'I'm Jessica Fletcher,' I said.

'I'm Officer Walsh. Coming with us?'

'Yes.'

Vaughan, Olga, and our dinner party accompanied me to the sidewalk. Everyone

225

else in the restaurant was aware of the commotion and strained to make sense of it.

'I'm coming with you,' Vaughan said.

'If you insist,' I said, opening the back door of Fred Mayer's taxi.

'In here, Mrs. Fletcher,' one of the officers said, indicating the back of his marked squad car.

'No,' I said. 'We'll follow.'

'What's going on?' Mayer asked. 'Am I in some sort of trouble?'

'No,' I said. Vaughan jumped in the taxi with me. 'Just follow the police car, Mr. Mayer.'

'Let me have those Tums,' he said, falling in behind the squad car. I handed them to him over the seat. The police vehicle turned on its flashing lights and siren, and picked up speed. Mayer kept pace, saying, 'At least I won't get a speeding ticket.'

We reached the town dock where a small gray building was surrounded with police cars, their swirling lights cutting through a dense fog, turning it into multicolored cotton candy. Vaughan and I got out of the taxi and were approached by Police Chief Cramer.

'He's in there?' I asked, pointing to the building.

'Yes.'

The harsh sound of a policeman's voice through a bullhorn violated the ears. 'Mr. Muller, this is the police. You are to come out with your hands up. You will not be hurt in any way. I promise you that. Just come out and everything will be fine.'

There was silence following what undoubtedly had been an oft-repeated announcement. I noticed a cop crouched by the door to the boathouse. He kept low as he ran back to where we stood. 'He says again he wants to talk to this Fletcher broad.'

The moment he said it, he saw me standing there. 'Are you—?'

'Yes. I'm that Fletcher broad. Don't let it bother you. I've been called worse.'

'Sorry, ma'am. It's just that—'

Chief Cramer cut him off. 'Are you willing to talk to him, Mrs. Fletcher?'

'That's why I'm here, Chief.'

'We'll escort you to the door. Talk to him through it.'

'What if he wants her to go inside?' Vaughan asked.

'That's up to her,' Cramer said, nodding at me.

'Let's see how it develops,' I said. 'Come on. I left a dinner that's getting cold.'

I was led to just outside the boathouse door. Uniformed cops with guns drawn flanked me. One of them nodded. I returned the nod.

'Hans?' I said in much too soft a voice. 'Hans?' Louder this time. 'Mr. Muller, it's Jessica Fletcher.'

We waited. There was no response.

'Mr. Muller. Are you in there?' I said, fairly

227

shouting this time.

Still no sound from inside.

'I'm going in,' I said.

'No, ma'am, not without the chief's order.' He looked back to where Cramer stood with Vaughan.

I instinctively reached for the door handle and turned it, pushed the door open. The only light inside was from the police cruisers that came and went in red bursts through a large skylight. I narrowed my eyes and saw a man's body on the floor. He was sitting up, his back propped against a wall.

I didn't hesitate. I stepped inside and went directly to the slumping body of Hans Muller. A handgun was on the floor a few feet from him. Next to it was a half-empty package of cigarettes, and a butt smoked down to its filtered end.

I came to his side and peered into his round face. I thought he was dead, but he proved me wrong by saying, 'Mrs. Fletcher. You came.' His breathing was labored, low rasps coming from his heaving chest. His beefy hand found mine.

'Yes, I came. Are you all right? Are you hurt?'

'Mrs. Fletcher, I did not kill that young girl.'

'No, I don't think you did.'

Police came through the door, flashlights illuminating us together on the floor. I held up my hand to keep them away. I said to Muller,

'Do you know how the model, Miki Dorsey, died?'

He coughed, sending his large body into spasm. He managed, '*Ya.*'

'Was it poison? Was it a poison called ricin?'

His answer was to squeeze my hand tightly, and then to let out an anguished, painful gasp. His free hand went to his chest. His eyes opened wide, filled with fear. 'It was—'

He shuddered. His grip on my hand loosened. A gurgling sound came from his throat. And he was still.

Suddenly, the damp, dank room was filled with police, their lights illuminating every corner. Chief Cramer knelt by Muller's lifeless body and touched the big German's neck in search of a pulse. There was none.

Using a handkerchief, an officer picked up the revolver and showed it to Cramer. The chief sniffed the end of the snub-nosed barrel. 'Hasn't been fired,' he said. He opened the chamber. 'Empty. No bullets.'

'What killed him?' I asked.

Vaughan Buckley came to where I stood and put his arm around me. He looked down at Muller and muttered, 'My God!'

As another policeman moved past us, his foot caught something on the concrete floor and sent it to the tip of my shoe. It was small, the size of a vitamin or pain-relieving gel. I picked it up and held it in my palm. It was a plastic ampoule that was broken in half. It reminded me of an electrical fuse of the type that's been replaced in most homes by circuit breakers.

'What do you have?' Vaughan asked.

I showed him.

'What is it?'

'I don't know, but I have a hunch.'

I showed the ampoule to Chief Cramer. He asked the same question Vaughan had asked.

'I think it might be what killed Hans Muller,' I said. 'Could you have what's left of the contents of this analyzed?'

'Sure. But why? What do you think it is?'

'Ricin.'

'Ricin?' Vaughan said.

'A poison, the same one that might have killed Miki Dorsey, and maybe Joshua Leopold.'

Cramer took the ampoule from me and placed it in a small plastic bag a uniformed officer handed him.

'What's in his pockets?' I asked.

'I'd rather wait for the crime-scene boys before anyone touched him.'

'Of course. His ever-present cigarettes are there,' I said, pointing to the package and the butt.

They were collected by an officer, and placed in plastic bags.

'That single butt, Chief Cramer. Remember the package of cigarettes I gave the coroner?'

'Yes?'

'Would you see to it that this butt is compared to the cigarettes in that package, the one I gave you?'

'Of course.'

'Am I free to leave now?'

'Sure. Will you see her home, Mr. Buckley?'

'Certainly. Come on, Jess.'

Fred Mayer stood next to his taxi as we approached. 'What's going on?' he asked.

'A death,' I replied.

'Back to Santa Fe Junction?' Vaughan asked. 'We left our dinners.'

'The last thing I want,' I said.

'We'll go to the house,' he said. 'No, first we'll swing by Scott's Inn and pick up your things. You're staying with us for the rest of your so-called vacation.'

'No, Vaughan, I don't want to impose. You have all that work going on and—'

'I'm your publisher, Jess, which makes me your boss in a sense. And your boss says you're staying with us.'

'All right,' I said, 'but I can't give up—I don't want to give up my room at the inn.'

'Why?'

'Because I might need to use it. I'll stay with you, but only with that caveat.'

'Fine. Mr. Mayer, first stop is Scott's Inn.'

CHAPTER TWENTY-FOUR

I took from my room at Scott's Inn only enough personal items for that night. Vaughan accompanied me to the room but didn't notice the second phone or the answering machine. The little red light on the machine wasn't flashing; no one had called.

We settled in the Buckleys' kitchen. I was hungry by this time; Vaughan put shell steaks on a gas barbecue on the patio, and Olga whipped up a simple salad.

'Delicious,' I said after we'd eaten.

'You have some constitution,' Olga said, 'being up for a meal after what you've been through tonight.'

'After what she's been through twice since arriving in the Hamptons,' said Vaughan.

'Three times,' I corrected. 'I was there when Miki Dorsey died.'

'Yes, three times,' Vaughan said. 'I'm sorry about all this, Jess. Somehow, I feel responsible by having invited you here.'

'Don't be silly.'

'Whether I'm responsible or not, tell me about this poison you think might have killed Hans.'

'Ricin?' I told them what I'd learned about it from George Sutherland.

'Whew!' Vaughan said. 'That's remarkable.'

232

'Hans had a background in intelligence, didn't he?' Olga said. 'With East Germany?'

Vaughan laughed. 'He talked about it. Frankly, I always considered it a case of fantasizing by Hans. You know, trying to inject intrigue into what was basically a pretty dull life.'

'Let's assume his background did include some sort of clandestine life,' I said. 'That would have given him access to a wide variety of things that kill.'

'True,' said Vaughan.

'But I have a problem,' I said.

'Which is?'

'Even if this potent poison, ricin, that I think was used to kill Miki Dorsey and perhaps Joshua Leopold, came from Hans Muller, I somehow can't buy him as having used it to murder anyone.'

'I never would have thought it, either, Jess,' Olga said.

'But if what I've pieced together is true—that there is a definite link between Muller, Maurice St. James, Blaine Dorsey—and if Miki Dorsey had been cut out of her role as Leopold's exclusive representative—and if Jo Ann Forbes had begun to put this together and lost her life because of it—then—'

Vaughan and Olga looked at me.

'Then *what*?' Vaughan asked.

'One of them is the murderer,' Olga said. 'Right, Jess?'

'Or someone murdering for them,' I said.

Olga made tea, and we sat on one of their screen porches. It had gotten warm and humid; the cicadas made their presence noisily known, harmony provided by an occasional cricket. It had been a clear night, but low clouds now obscured the moon and stars.

We didn't say much as we sat in the dark. I suppose we each were dealing with our individual thoughts and reactions to what by now had become a pattern of death in the pretty, pleasant Hamptons. Hans Muller had been their friend, and now he was dead, probably of a poison he administered to himself, the same poison that perhaps had killed Miki Dorsey. But that was supposition on my part. A second autopsy on her was crucial to proving my thesis.

Vaughan, who'd left the kitchen and the porch a few times to take phone calls in his study, broke the silence: 'I know one thing for certain, Jess.'

'Yes?'

'If you thought there was media interest in you before, this nasty episode with Hans tonight will make your life hell.'

I nodded in agreement. He was right, of course. I didn't relish the thought.

I eventually excused myself and went to the pretty guest room above their three-car garage. Olga had laid out fresh towels for me and a small basket of pretty-smelling soaps.

How she came up with fresh flowers on such short notice was a mystery to me, but she had.

I got ready for bed, and was about to turn out the light when I saw that there was a phone in the room. I hesitated picking it up in case someone was on the line. But I did, and received a dial tone. I pulled the slip of paper from my purse on which was written the number of the new phone in my room at Scott's Inn and dialed it.

'You have reached—'

The moment I heard my voice begin to give the outgoing message, I punched in '1,' then '0.' My message stopped. A mechanical male voice said, *'You have one message.'*

I heard the tape rewind. And then a man's voice said: *'I understand you wish to buy a sketch by a certain famous woman. I have that sketch. I will call again.'*

There was a 'beep,' and all went quiet.

I hung up and tried to place the man's voice. I failed. I detected the hint of a Southern accent. I also had the feeling the voice was being disguised in some way; the old place-a-handkerchief-over-the-mouthpiece routine? I was tempted to tap into the message again but decided it could wait until morning.

Sleep came later, and with some difficulty. I assume I dreamed, but had no recollection when I awoke in the morning to birds singing and sunlight streaming through the windows, what those dreams might have been.

I used the phone to call Fred Mayer's little office across from police headquarters. I'd told him I'd let him know when I needed him that day.

'Morning, Mrs. Fletcher. Just sitting here listening to the news about that fella last night down at the town dock.'

'What are they saying?' I asked.

'Seems he was a German guy. Maybe a spy. The announcer says the cops suspect suicide.'

'What else was said?'

'Just that you were there, a regular heroine, going inside to try and save him.'

'That's not what I did. Can you pick me up at Mr. Buckley's house in an hour?'

'Yes, ma'am, provided I can get the cab out of the driveway.'

'Why would that be a problem?'

'Got to be a dozen cars and trucks belonging to newspapers and radio stations and the like. Seems they know I'm your driver and intend to follow me.'

'I'm sorry.'

He laughed. 'Hey, don't be sorry. Most excitement I've had in thirty years. Be there in an hour.'

Should I cancel him, and try to avoid the press by using other means of transportation?

No. They'd find me no matter how I elected to get around.

'Yes,' I said. 'An hour.'

CHAPTER TWENTY-FIVE

I felt like I was in a parade.

I sat in the back of Fred Mayer's taxi as we led an entourage of media vehicles from the Buckley house into town. Vaughan and Olga had urged me to lay low, to use their pool and tennis court, to lounge about and read, nap, relax. Although a hoard of workmen had descended at eight, Vaughan assured me they would not be hammering and sawing everywhere, and that I could find spots of solitude and relative silence.

I knew they meant well; the contemplation of what they suggested was appealing.

But I was determined to move the day along, and to take every step that might help that process.

I ran into Scott's Inn, where Mr. Scott was at his desk.

'Good morning,' I said.

'Good morning, Mrs. Fletcher.' He gave me a wry smile. 'Looks like you just seem to attract murder.'

'Goodness, I hope that's not true,' I said as he handed me a batch of message slips, which I didn't bother to read. 'Besides, the gentleman who died last night wasn't murdered. He committed suicide.'

The moment I said it, it flashed across my

mind that maybe Hans Muller *hadn't* committed suicide. Could someone else have been in the boathouse and used ricin to kill him?

I went upstairs and listened to the message again. I played it over and over. There was something vaguely familiar, but I still couldn't identify who owned the voice.

I called Police Chief Cramer.

'Mrs. Fletcher, I'm glad you called.'

'I thought I'd better check in.'

'You should know you're not alone in this.'

'Why do you say that?'

'I just got off the phone with a Sheriff Morton Metzger from Cabot Cove.'

'You *did*? Why did Mort call *you*?'

'He says he heard about last night from TV news, and wanted me to know that he was holding me and my department personally accountable if anything happens to you.'

'He didn't *really* say that?'

'Yes, he did. Actually, he sounded like a nice fellow. I'm sure he meant well.'

'Mort is a—nice fellow. He means well. Have you heard from Dr. Eder?'

'He called just before your sheriff friend did. Called from the city. Those cigarettes you gave him are being analyzed as we speak. He says the forensic scientist knows a lot about this ricin you think might be in them.'

'Good. What about a second autopsy on Miki Dorsey?'

'Should know for certain by noon. I think it's pretty well decided. There's some heavy influence being peddled on that issue.'

'So you said. What about her father?'

'Went back to London last night.'

'I wish he hadn't done that.'

'Why?'

'Just a feeling.'

'You have lots of those, Mrs. Fletcher.'

'I suppose I do. A family curse. I don't suppose you have any new information on Mr. Muller.'

'Dr. Eder is doing an autopsy this afternoon as soon as he gets back from the city.'

'What was in his pockets?'

'You asked that last night. I have an inventory. I can get it for you.'

'Could I come by and see it?'

'Any time. I plan to be here most of the day.'

I emerged from Scott's Inn into the crowd of press people who'd followed me there. They started shooting questions at me. I paused at the top of the steps leading to the porch, held up my hands, and said, 'I am going shopping. Then, I intend to enjoy a quiet lunch—*alone*.'

The number of questions tripled, all having to do with my having been present in the boathouse last night. I waited patiently until the din died down, then said, 'Ladies and gentlemen, you are chasing the wrong person. I am here in the Hamptons to enjoy a much-needed vacation. A few unfortunate events

239

have gotten in the way of that. I don't intend to allow any other distractions to interfere with my leisure during my final days here. I will say nothing else to you, and I would appreciate being left alone. Thank you.'

As I settled in the rear seat of Mayer's taxi, a female reporter asked him where he was taking me next.

Mayer laughed: 'With this lady, you never know.' He turned to me. 'Where to, Mrs. Fletcher?'

'A shop that sells clocks.'

'Clocks?' the reporter said through the open window.

'Clocks,' I repeated, tapping Mayer on the shoulder. He slowly pulled away, leaving a puzzled reporter. A few cars fell in behind us, but I was pleased that most did not.

'You serious about a store that sells clocks?' Mayer asked.

'Absolutely.'

'I know just the place.'

*   *   *

I stuck to my announced plan to shop, and to enjoy a quiet lunch until four o'clock—and until the few reporters following me eventually gave up—which, of course, was what I intended to happen.

During lunch, which I enjoyed on the terrace of the Post House, a lovely restaurant recommended by Mayer, I used a phone inside to call Maurice St. James at his gallery.

'Mr. St. James, have you come up with something to show me?' I asked.

'Mrs. Fletcher. I didn't expect to hear from you today. Not with what has happened to Hans.'

'Poor man,' I said.

'You were there.' He didn't add *as usual*.

'Yes, I was.'

'He killed himself?'

'Evidently. Maurice, I plan to leave the Hamptons very soon. Do you have works to show me?'

'I have. It wasn't easy, but I think you'll be pleased with what you see.'

'Wonderful. When can we meet?'

'The gallery usually closes at nine today, but I'll close earlier. Say seven?'

'I'll be there.'

'Come to the back. Discretion is very much in order.'

'I understand.'

Back at Scott's Inn, I went to my room and unwrapped my purchases of that afternoon, including the clock for Seth Hazlitt. It was exactly what he wanted.

The red message light on the answering machine flickered indicating a message. There were two. The first was from Waldine Peckham: *This is Wally Peckham, Mrs. Fletcher. I think I've done pretty much everything*

I can. Any luck so far?'
The second was the same male voice I'd heard earlier. He said: *'I call again to offer the sketch you wish to buy. I will call one more time, tonight at midnight. If I fail to reach you, I won't call again.'*

I made a mental note to be there at twelve, or lose the opportunity to recover my missing sketch.

Next stop, police headquarters.

'Well, Mrs. Fletcher, looks like you're getting everything you've asked for.'

'I'm pleased to hear that. What about the tests for ricin?'

'You were right. There was ricin in that one cigarette butt that was smoked by Ms. Dorsey just prior to her death. And the ampoule you found at the scene of Mr. Muller's death also contained traces of the poison.'

I'd held my breath after asking the question. Now, with my gut instincts scientifically validated, I exhaled.

Chief Cramer smiled. 'You should be pleased, Mrs. Fletcher.'

'Oh, I am. I certainly am. Will the second autopsy on Miki Dorsey take place?'

'First thing in the morning. Dr. Eder is examining Hans Muller now. He told me he picked up quite a bit of knowledge from his forensic scientist friend in the city. He'll be looking closely for any traces of ricin in Muller's body.'

'Good.'

'So far. But there's a large question remaining.'

'I'm well aware of that,' I said. 'Who killed Miki Dorsey and Jo Ann Forbes? And—'

'And what?'

'Maybe who killed Joshua Leopold, and possibly Hans Muller? Any chance of exhuming Leopold's body?'

'Now that it looks like ricin killed Ms. Dorsey, case could be made to take another look at Leopold's body. I'll see what I can do to put that into motion.'

'I appreciate it, Chief.'

'In the meantime, how are things with you?'

'Just fine. I finally found some time to rest and relax. I did some shopping and had a delicious lunch.'

'It's about time. Anything further I can do for you?'

'Thank you, no. You've done so much already. But I will touch base with you regularly.'

'Always delighted to hear from you. And thanks again to you and your Scotland Yard friend for coming up with the ricin theory.'

'I'll pass your thanks along to George.'

I spent the time between leaving Chief Cramer's office and returning to Scott's Inn making notes. I've always been an inveterate note maker, whether it's a shopping list, a page of notes on what I intend to accomplish in any given day, or simply to help me focus my thoughts. That was something I tried to get across to my students in the seminar at NYU—that the act of writing forces you to think more clearly, about anything and everything.

My pen-and-paper exercise was interrupted a number of times by calls. Mort Metzger called from Cabot Cove to repeat to me his message to Chief Cramer.

'I know you care about me, Mort, but there's no need to call the police here.'

'Mrs. F., when I heard you were at the scene of another sudden death, I knew I had to make that call. Let the police handle things. You get home here and write your books. You're a writer, not a cop.'

'You're absolutely right.'

'Of course I am. And Seth agrees with me.'

We chatted for a few more minutes before ending our conversation.

Waldine Peckham called a few minutes after Mort and I hung up. I told her that her efforts seemed to have paid off, and recounted the two messages recorded on the answering machine. She was her characteristic low-key self: 'I hope it works, but it probably won't.'

I thanked her again for her help, and promised to let her know how things progressed.

Vaughan Buckley called as I was preparing to leave for Maurice St. James's gallery. 'Free for dinner?' he asked.

'No, Vaughan. I decided to relax today. Did some shopping, bought a gift for a friend. I'm planning a quiet night.'

'Great. I'll pick you up in ten minutes.'

'Why?'

'You're staying with us. Remember?'

'Oh, Vaughan, now that I'm off the case, as it were, and devoting myself strictly to rest and relaxation, I much prefer to stay here at the inn. You and Olga are wonderful to care so much about me, but I'm happy and secure right here.'

'I wish you'd reconsider.'

'But I won't. You and that knockout of a wife of yours go out and enjoy the evening. I'll be asleep by ten.'

'I know better than to argue with you. Check in with us in the morning?'

'Absolutely.'

I'd dismissed Fred Mayer for the evening because he said he and his wife were having friends over. I now considered him a friend. He was a delightful gentleman, easygoing and unfailingly pleasant. I sensed after my lunch at the Post House that he might have taken a drink or two at some nearby pub. But I didn't raise it with him. He drove sensibly for the rest of the afternoon, and wished me a pleasant evening before dropping me off.

Time for my appointment with Maurice St. James.

I went to the gallery's rear as instructed and

245

knocked on the metal door. It was dark back there, and I was grateful when St. James responded quickly. I looked past him. A narrow, dark hallway led into the rear of the gallery.

'Please, come in.'

The door closed behind me with a harsh clang. I followed St. James down the hall and into the gallery itself. Tiny pin spots trained on certain Leopold works provided dim light for the entire space.

'Is what you're showing me on the walls?' I asked. 'I've already seen these.'

'No. But before we get to the business at hand, I must ask you something, Mrs. Fletcher.'

'Yes?'

'Are you—well, Mrs. Fletcher, I must be assured that you are a legitimate buyer.'

'Of course I am. I'm—'

He raised his hand against my words. 'Some of these works I am about to offer you, Mrs. Fletcher, have an unconventional provenance.'

'Meaning?'

'Meaning that they've come into my possession from a variety of sources, not all of them—legitimate.'

'I wasn't aware of that,' I said.

He held up his hand and smiled. 'I am not saying that *I* have engaged in illegitimate activities. I would never stoop to that. But I did feel it appropriate to raise the subject with you.'

'And I appreciate it, Maurice. Now that I'm forewarned, let's get on with it. I'm not uncomfortable with the situation.'

He rubbed his hands. 'Good. Splendid. Come.'

The room he led me to was one I wasn't aware existed. It was fairly large. Two wooden worktables dominated the center. Lights with green metal shades were suspended above them.

'This is our framing and preparation room,' St. James said. 'It hasn't been used much recently. Business has been slow.'

'The economy?'

'Among other things. Of course, that we feature only Joshua Leopold makes it more difficult.'

'I understand,' I said. 'Now, could we—?'

'Of course. I'm sorry. I just feel a need to explain why I am willing to do certain things. Here.'

He went to a corner where a pile of something was covered by a white cloth. He stripped the cloth away, revealing dozens of framed paintings leaning against each other. He picked up the first of them, carried it to where I stood next to a table, and held it up to catch the light.

It was a typical Leopold; I'd now seen enough of them in the gallery to recognize his style. But then I thought of Chris Turi's paintings in the studio where Leopold had died a year ago. Would I be able to discern the difference between him and Josh Leopold? I answered myself: No.

'When was this painted?' I asked. 'I mean, at what stage in his career?'

'Late in his career, Mrs. Fletcher. I would say, oh, perhaps six months before he died. Do you like it?'

'Very much. Where has it been for the past year?'

'In private hands. Let me show you another.'

Twenty minutes later, St. James had shown me two dozen paintings attributed to Joshua Leopold.

'Well,' he said after the last painting had been exhibited for my approval. 'Which ones appeal most?'

'Hard to say,' I said. 'I'm afraid I'll have to look at them again.'

'Certainly. Let me prop them up around the room. That way, you'll be better able to compare.'

As he spread out the paintings, I moved to where another white cloth covered something on the opposite side of the room. I pulled the cover back and saw another stack of paintings. The first one in the row immediately caught my eye. It had been rendered with a palette knife, vivid, bold colors slashing across the canvas. In the lower left was a crude cubist rendition of a nude young woman seated on a stool, her head and hair hanging down between her knees.

I'd seen that painting before. In the studio shared by Chris Turi and Carlton Wells. I crouched and leaned closer to read the artist's signature. *Joshua Leopold.*

As I straightened up, I felt St. James's presence immediately behind. I turned. His thin face was somber and cold.

'May I see these?' I said.

'Those are new, Mrs. Fletcher. I haven't had time to evaluate their worth.'

'New? Leopold's been dead over a year.'

His reply was to cover the second set of paintings again, move to the center of the room, and say, 'Which ones do you wish to buy, Mrs. Fletcher? I have another appointment.'

'How much are they?'

'They vary in price. But for you—if you buy six or more—one hundred thousand dollars. Cash.'

'May I have overnight to think it over?'

'If you must. Be here at nine tomorrow morning. Otherwise, the offer is withdrawn.'

'I understand. Maurice, let me be direct with you. You, Hans Muller, and, I believe, Miki Dorsey's father, Blaine Dorsey, have been involved in promoting the name of Joshua Leopold and selling his works.'

His face said nothing.

'You *are* aware that Miki Dorsey was murdered?'

Now his face said much. His eyes widened, and his mouth twisted into a thin, severe line.

'She was poisoned by something called ricin.'

'I know nothing of what you're talking about.'

'Oh, I think you do, Maurice. I believe Hans Muller died from that same poison.'

He stiffened, looking to me as though he didn't know what to say or what to do next. Finally, he managed, 'You aren't interested in buying these works. Are you?'

'I said I needed to think about it overnight.'

'You're here because you think I have done something wrong.'

I pointed to the second pile of paintings. 'Isn't having forgeries made and sold to an unsuspecting public "doing something wrong"?'

Until that moment, I'd felt secure in being direct with Maurice St. James. But then he picked up a knife with a curved blade I assumed was used in the framing process, and idly passed it from hand to hand. As he did, he moved in the direction of the door.

'I have to leave now,' I said. 'I'll get back to you by nine.'

His expression remained stone-like.

I stepped in his direction.

'You misunderstand, Mrs. Fletcher. You misunderstand.'

I tensed; was he about to lunge at me with the knife?

A car's horn was heard from the street.

'That's my driver,' I said.

'Your driver?'

'Yes. Thank you. I'll get back to you.'

He stepped aside, and I left through the back door. A sound just across the narrow alley caused me to jump. I looked into the shadows but saw nothing. Probably a cat.

I walked quickly to the street, turning in a direction that would not afford him a view of whether or not I did, in fact, have someone waiting for me.

My heart pounded. He'd frightened me once he picked up the knife. I now knew that there was an underground market in forged Joshua Leopold art, and that Chris Turi was, at least, one of those turning out the forgeries.

But how did that link up with murder?

I was confident that the autopsy on Hans Muller would confirm he died from ricin, and it was now established that Miki Dorsey died from it. And I suspected Joshua Leopold had, too.

Muller would have been the only possible source of the poison, by virtue of his former connection with East German intelligence.

But who had used ricin on Miki Dorsey?

Hans Muller? I somehow doubted it.

Maurice St. James? A good possibility.

Blaine Dorsey? Her own father? He was in

London when she died. Wasn't he? But had he known, along with the others, about the scam being perpetrated in forged art? And if Leopold himself had been murdered, with ricin the cause, had Blaine Dorsey known about that, too? And been involved in Leopold's death?

Carlton Wells? Anne Harris and Waldine Peckham both had questions about him because of his former relationship with Miki.

It occurred to me as I continued to walk away from the gallery that I'd been blithely ignoring others who'd lived with Miki in the group house. I really knew only two, Anne Harris and Wally Peckham.

And there was Jo Ann Forbes, the vibrant reporter for *Dan's Papers,* found dead in Muller's cottage. Had he killed her? Now that he was dead, it was unlikely anyone would ever know with certainty. Her notes said to me that she was on to something having to do with the Joshua Leopold art scam. Was that why she was killed? I thought so.

I circled back to Scott's Inn and went to my room. It was eight-thirty. I hadn't eaten but wasn't hungry. I was still slightly shaken by the way my meeting with St. James had gone. I knew I had to be in my room at midnight to receive the call from the person selling my sketch of the naked male model. The question was what to do between now and then.

I was looking out the window when it struck

me that I'd forgotten to ask Police Chief Hopeful Cramer an important question. I tried him at headquarters, but was told he'd gone home for the night. The officer on duty didn't hesitate to give me the chief's home number: 'I know he wouldn't mind you having it, Mrs. Fletcher.'

Cramer's wife answered. I introduced myself. After some pleasant chat, he came on the line.

'Sorry to bother you at home, Chief, but I forgot to ask you something this afternoon.'

'Sure. Go ahead and ask.'

And I did.

CHAPTER TWENTY-SIX

I'd no sooner hung up on Chief Cramer when the newly installed phone rang.

'Mrs. Fletcher, it's Anne Harris.'

'Hello, Anne. I was hoping to hear from you.'

'Are you alone?'

'Yes. Why do you ask?'

'I was wondering whether we could get together.'

'Tonight?'

'Yes, if you're not busy.'

'I'm not. But I do have to be back here by midnight for a call.'

She laughed. 'You sound like Cinderella. I'll have you back long before that. Pick you up. Ten minutes?'

'All right. I'll be waiting downstairs.'

As I stood on the porch, I became increasingly anxious to see her and talk with her again. She'd said my first night at the group house that there was more to Miki Dorsey's death than met the eye. Maybe this was the night she'd explain what she'd meant.

I asked where we were going once we pulled away from Scott's Inn.

'Back to the house, if that's okay with you.'

'Fine. How has everything been with you?'

'Pretty good.'

'Anne, you called on a number I've given only to two other people.'

'Oh?'

'Where did you get it?'

'Wally.'

'She told you?'

'Yup.'

If that were true, I'd lost some faith in Waldine Peckham.

We pulled into the driveway, got out, and went inside the house. There were no sounds. The only light came from the living room. I followed Anne down the dark hallway until we reached the room commonly shared by all the house's summer residents.

'Beer, Mrs. Fletcher? Coke?'

'A diet drink would be fine.'

She went to get it, and I casually strolled the room. A cello on a stand in one corner, undoubtedly belonging to Anne. I'd forgotten she'd said she was a musician.

In another corner, near French doors that were cracked open, was a half-finished painting on an easel, probably the work of Waldine Peckham.

'Is Wally here?' I asked when Anne reappeared.

'I don't know. I don't keep track of her.'

Her comment had a nasty edge to it, which surprised me. Evidently, Waldine Peckham and Anne Harris weren't the best of friends.

She handed me my soda and sat on the window seat. I wasn't sure where to perch, so I continued standing. When she didn't say anything, I said, 'I've been wanting to speak with you ever since the first night I was here. I don't know if you're aware that I've been spending some time looking into Miki Dorsey's death. Jo Ann Forbes's, too. And now Hans Muller's.'

She said nothing, simply sat and stared into her coffee cup. I joined her on the window seat. 'Anne, tell me what it is you know.'

She drew a breath, turned, and locked eyes with me. 'There are certain things that have been going on out here for the past couple of years which have gotten lots of people in trouble.'

'In trouble? What do you mean?'

'Have gotten them killed.'

I nodded. 'Go on.'

I could see her internal debate swirling inside her—to tell me more, or to stop.

'Anne, I never had any intention of becoming involved in murder when I came to the Hamptons for a vacation. It's hardly been that. But I happened to be in an art class when Miki Dorsey died. Because of that, I got to know a local reporter, Jo Ann Forbes, and she ended up dead, too. And then someone I met socially, Hans Muller, ends up dead. All I want is to leave here knowing that justice has been done. For Miki. For Jo Ann. And for Mr. Muller.'

'I can understand that,' she said.

'Do you know that Miki didn't die of a heart attack?'

'Yes. She was poisoned.'

'That's right. But how did you know that?'

'I—'

'Who told you?'

'I did, Mrs. Fletcher.'

Maurice St. James stepped from the dark recesses of the kitchen.

His sudden and unexpected appearance on the scene startled me. Again, I saw a vision of the curved knife in his hands. He held nothing in them now.

I asked Anne Harris, 'Why did you bring me here?' my voice steady and hard.

'To make sure you stay out of our way long

enough for us to accomplish what we must,' said St. James.

'Which is?' I asked, forcing an increasing fear from my voice.

'To put an end to what has been going on,' Anne Harris said. 'I'm sure you'd like to see that happen.'

'Not without those responsible for the deaths of four people brought to justice.'

'Four?' St. James said.

'Yes. Miki Dorsey. Poisoned. Jo Ann Forbes. Beaten to death. Hans Muller. Poisoned. Joshua Leopold. Poisoned.'

'You have a rich imagination, Mrs. Fletcher,' St. James said. 'But that is to be expected from a writer of murder mysteries.'

'It's not my imagination, Maurice. But I must admit, Anne, that I never thought you were a part of this nasty little game.'

'That doesn't matter. Besides, I haven't killed anyone. That's the truth.'

'But you're supporting those who have, and you brought me here tonight under false pretenses, to get me out of the way until—what? Until you're able to pack up and leave?'

'You're very astute, Mrs. Fletcher,' St. James said. 'We're not asking much of you. You've been poking your pretty nose into things that are none of your business. Because you have, it's necessary for us to make alternate plans.'

I stood and walked to the center of the

room. Neither Anne Harris nor Maurice St. James moved to stop me. I had a moment of exhilaration. Maybe they weren't ready to back up their threatening words with action.

But as I took another step in the direction of the hall leading to the front of the house, I heard the front door open, then slam closed. Moments later, Carlton Wells joined us in the living room, blocking my exit.

I took everyone in. It was a cabal, this dealing in forged art—and murder. Who wasn't involved? Waldine Peckham? Chris Turi? I wouldn't have been surprised to see them join the crowd any moment.

I decided that my only option was to stand tall and firm. Of course, if these people had killed the others, that stance might end up nothing more than foolhardy bravado. But I didn't see any alternative.

'I don't know all the details of what you've done, or how you've done it,' I said, 'but if you've been responsible for the deaths of these people, you'll never be able to run away from it. Your only sensible course of action is to—'

'Why don't you shut up!' Carlton Wells stepped closer to me and thrust his jaw at me. 'You're a meddling old fool, lady. None of this is your business, so just shut up unless you—'

I cut him off with, 'Unless I want to be murdered, too? Let me ask you something, Mr. Wells. Was the money you've all made from selling Joshua Leopold paintings—and forged copies of them—worth murder?'

'Just sit down over there,' Wells said, pointing to a chair near the entrance to the kitchen. I stood my ground. He grabbed my arm and propelled me to the chair. His grip was powerful; I winced against the pain it caused. 'I'm going back to finish packing up, Maurice,' he said. 'I need help.'

'What about her?' St. James asked, referring to me.

'Get some rope and tie her up.'

I stood.

Wells pushed me back down in the chair.

I looked to Anne Harris, who stood with her back to the action, arms crossed, her attention focused on a window and what was outside it.

'Anne,' I said, 'they may not have any common sense, but certainly you do. It's not too late for you to—'

She turned, said to Wells and St. James, 'Give me the gun. I'll make sure she doesn't go anywhere.'

Wells drew a small snub-nosed revolver from his windbreaker pocket and handed it to her. To me: 'Just keep your mouth shut, Mrs. Fletcher, and you'll be all right—for now.'

I watched St. James and Wells leave the room and disappear down the hall. I turned to Anne, who had now taken a chair a few feet from me. The revolver rested comfortably in her hands—too comfortable, I thought. This seemingly sweet, pleasant woman obviously had another hard, vicious side to her.

We sat in silence, eyes on each other. Finally, I said, 'Anne, I know you didn't kill Miki Dorsey, or anyone else for that matter. I know who did.'

Her eyebrows lifted slightly. 'Oh?' she said, a tiny smile on her lips.

'But if you go along with them, you'll end up being tossed right in the midst of murder charges. You're so young. Why would you want to throw away your life?'

'I don't have a choice, Mrs. Fletcher.'

'Of course you do.' I leaned forward as I said it to amplify my words, but my action caused her to stiffen, and to lift the weapon and point it at me.

I averted my gaze from the revolver and looked directly at her face. 'I don't know the extent of your involvement in this enterprise, Anne, but my instincts tell me—and they're usually pretty good—that you're a minor player.'

Her face took on sudden animation. Her laugh was scornful. 'Maybe your instincts aren't as wonderful as you think they are,' she said.

'Maybe they aren't. But I prefer to go with them.'

Her animated face changed from wide-eyed wonder to a dark, serious frown. 'Do you know how much money can be made from an artist like Josh Leopold, Mrs. Fletcher?'

260

'I'm afraid I've started to learn.'

'He's the hottest young artist on the scene today.'

'But he's dead.'

A guffaw. 'And worth a lot more dead than alive.'

Her message wasn't lost on me: 'Are you saying he was *killed* in order to increase his worth on the open art market?'

'That, and other reasons. He started out going along with having other artists paint under his name. It's no big deal. Every great artist had apprentices who painted in their style. How many masterpieces hanging in museums today were actually painted by the masters' apprentices? A lot more than you think.'

'But he balked, and died for it.'

'Why don't we stop talking, Mrs. Fletcher. It won't get either of us anywhere.' She lowered the revolver to her lap and sat back.

As she did, I saw a shadow move across the wall behind her. The source of the shadow became visible. It was Wally Peckham who stepped through the open set of French doors. She picked up a wooden palette by her easel and continued toward us. I kept my eyes on Anne to avoid tipping her that someone else was in the room.

Wally silently crossed the room and came up behind Anne. Anne finally realized someone was there, but reacted too slowly. Wally

261

brought the edge of the palette down across the back of Anne's neck. Simultaneously, I leaped up and grabbed the weapon from her.

Anne slumped in the chair, her eyes closed, her hand gripping her neck and back of her head. Wally stood frozen next to me. We heard each other's hard breathing, and felt our mutual trembling.

Anne looked up at us. 'Bitch!' she said to Wally.

'Let's go, Mrs. Fletcher,' Wally said. 'I think it's time to get out of here.'

'What about Anne?' I asked.

'Forget her. She's not worth worrying about.'

Anne slowly got to her feet. Her expressive face was now a mask of pity and sorrow. She began to cry. 'Mrs. Fletcher, you were right. I never killed anyone. I got involved—I mean, I didn't want to get involved but—'

I stopped her mea culpa speech. 'Anne, you'll have a chance to explain to the proper authorities. In the meantime, you can help me, which might work in your favor.'

'I never meant—'

'Stop it! Where have Carlton and Maurice gone?'

'To the gallery to pack up the paintings.'

'And where are they going after that?'

'Europe. They already have their tickets. Once you started uncovering things, they decided it was time to pack up and get out.'

'Where in Europe?'

'London. Blaine Dorsey is part of the group.'

'But his daughter was killed.'

'Let's go, Mrs. Fletcher,' Wally said, yanking on my arm.

'All right. My suggestion to you, Anne, is that you stay right here.'

She didn't reply. Wally tugged at me again, and we ran up the hall and out the front door.

'Where's your car?' I asked.

'I don't have one. You?'

'I don't drive.'

I looked to my left. Two bikes leaned against the porch. 'Ride a bike?' I asked.

'Not since I was a kid.'

'You never forget. I ride them all the time back home. Come on.'

They were men's bikes, and not in very good shape. I told Wally she was the navigator back to Scott's Inn: 'The fastest way you know,' I said.

She led us through backyards and up tiny streets. I began to wonder whether she knew where she was going, but suddenly we were at the rear of the inn's property, and entering through the gate leading to the English garden. We dropped the bikes to the ground and tried the rear door. It was locked. We skirted the inn and came in through the front door. 'Come on,' I said. 'My room's upstairs.'

We were about to ascend the stairs when

Mr. Scott came through a door and said, 'Mrs. Fletcher. There's someone to see you.' As he said it, Chris Turi came from the library.

'Chris,' Wally said.

'Hi. I got here as fast as I could.'

Wally and I looked at each other.

'I heard you were at Maurice's gallery, Mrs. Fletcher, and that you told him everything you knew. You're in danger.'

'Maurice told you?' I asked.

'Yeah.'

'Have you spoken with Anne Harris?'

'No. Come on. I have a car. I'll take you to the police.'

'Yes, you'll be going to the police, Chris. To be charged with the murder of Miki Dorsey, Jo Ann Forbes, and Hans Muller. And maybe Joshua Leopold.'

'What the hell are you talking about?'

'You killed them, Chris, to keep them quiet. Miki knew from the beginning about the scheme to forge and sell art under Leopold's name. She was his representative until you and your greedy friends took that away from her. You couldn't blame her for being angry and threatening to blow the whistle.'

He looked as though he might lunge at me. But he stayed where he was and glared.

'Jo Ann Forbes, good journalist that she was, was piecing together everything, and that got her killed, too. What did you do, Chris, have Hans Muller lure her to his cottage with

264

the promise of giving her information? Mr. Muller may not have been the most sterling of characters—providing the poison for you to kill Josh Leopold and Miki Dorsey wasn't a very nice thing to do—but he didn't have the guts to kill anyone himself. And he didn't have to, because you were there to take care of it.'

Turi looked around the room. Mr. Scott had disappeared. Wally Peckham looked at Chris with her usual noncommittal expression.

I continued: 'And then Muller had to go because he couldn't take the heat of being the prime suspect in Jo Ann Forbes's murder. He was a weak man, wasn't he, Chris?'

'I don't have to listen to this,' Turi said.

'You came here to kill again, didn't you?' I said. 'This time I was to be the victim.'

He moved toward the front door. As he did, sirens and flashing lights erupted from the street. Joe Scott reappeared, saying to me, 'I thought we could use the police here, Mrs. Fletcher.'

Chief Hopeful Cramer, who led four uniformed officers through the door, went directly to Wally Peckham. 'Nice job, Wally,' he said, grinning. A small smile came from her.

My puzzled expression prompted him to add, 'Ms. Peckham has been a valuable help in breaking this art forgery ring.'

She shrugged.

'I'm afraid there's a lot of explaining to be done,' I said.

'Happy to do it,' said the chief, 'now that this is over.'

'But it isn't,' I said. 'Maurice St. James and Carlton Wells are cleaning out the gallery of forged Leopold paintings.'

'No they're not. Those paintings are being loaded into police vehicles as we speak, along with St. James and Wells.'

Chris Turi looked like a cornered animal. I pointed to him and said, 'He's your murderer, Chief, with plenty of accomplices.'

'I figured that, Mrs. Fletcher, after the results came back on the cigarette butt found next to Muller's body, and you explained to me the significance of it.' He said to his officers, 'Arrest him.'

Turi broke for the door, but was grabbed, his arms brought behind his back and cuffs slapped on his wrists.

If looks could kill, I was dead. Turi glared at me, daggers flying from his eyes. I said, 'You should have gotten the message, Chris.'

'What message?'

'That smoking can be hazardous to your health.'

As they led Turi away, I asked Wally Peckham, 'What time is it?'

'Quarter of twelve,' she said.

'Excuse us,' I said, pulling her in the direction of the stairs. We went to my room and checked the answering machine. No message.

'He said he'd call again at midnight?' Wally asked.

'Yes. You certainly succeeded in getting the word out that there was a serious buyer for my sketch of the male model.'

'Not hard in the Hamptons. Tell one person and everybody knows.'

At precisely midnight, the newly installed phone rang. Wally and I looked at each other. 'Answer it,' she said.

'Hello?'

'Jess?'

'Vaughan?'

'Hope I didn't wake you.'

My laugh was involuntary and loud. 'No, Vaughan, you didn't wake me. As a matter of fact, I was sitting here by the phone waiting for a call.'

'At this hour?' He realized he was calling at 'this hour' and laughed. 'I take it you want me to get off.'

'If you don't mind. I'll call you back.'

But there was no call. Not by twelve-fifteen. Not by twelve-thirty.

We went downstairs where Joe Scott handed me a note left by Police Chief Cramer, asking me to call him first thing in the morning.

I walked to the porch with Wally Peckham. We stood silently, each deep in our own thoughts. I broke the silence. 'You were working for the police?'

'Yup.'

'From before I even met you?'

'Yup.'

'I wish I'd known.'

'Better you didn't. Chief Cramer and I discussed letting you in on it once you started uncovering things. We agreed it was better not to.'

'Why?'

'For one thing, it might have jeopardized my situation.'

'I wouldn't have said anything.'

'Couldn't take the chance.'

'Was there a second reason?'

'Yup.'

'And?'

'Chief Cramer felt you were doing so well, he didn't want to discourage you.'

'Uh-huh.'

'I want to get back to the house. It's past my bedtime.'

'What about Anne?'

'The chief was sending cops to pick her up. I'll be fine. You?'

'Fine.'

I called Vaughan the minute I returned to my room. We talked briefly. I wasn't up to telling him about the evening's events, so just said I was tired and needed some sleep. We agreed to meet for breakfast at nine.

*   *   *

'Incredible,' he said after we'd enjoyed breakfast, and I'd told him everything. 'I had no idea you were so up to your neck in this thing.'

'Well, Vaughan, I was, but it's over. I'm glad it is.'

I'd called Chief Cramer before leaving Scott's Inn to meet Vaughan, and made an appointment to see him that morning.

'Mind if I tag along?' Vaughan asked.

'Not at all.'

The chief was in an expansive mood when we arrived. He told us he'd been investigating the forged art ring for almost a year, and had recruited Wally Peckham after she came to him with what she knew of the St. James—Muller—Blaine Dorsey—Chris Turi—Carlton Wells enterprise. She was an insider in the group house, which made her invaluable.

He took us into a conference room where more than two hundred paintings confiscated from Maurice St. James's gallery the night before were propped against the walls. I recognized some from having been shown them in St. James's framing room.

One immediately caught Vaughan's eye. It was the painting Hans Muller had taken from his house the night of the dinner party. 'He had it all along,' he said, holding up the painting for us to see, and explaining to Cramer that the work belonged to him.

'I'll have to keep it for a while, Vaughan. It's evidence.'

'I understand,' Vaughan said.

'There's one piece I won't have to keep, however,' said the chief.

'Which is?' I asked.

'This.'

He pulled from behind a framed canvas my missing sketch of the nude male model. 'I believe this belongs to you, Mrs. Fletcher,' he said, handing it to me.

'Yes. It's my sketch.'

'Let me see,' Vaughan said, reaching.

I withheld it from him. 'No,' I said. 'No one sees this except me.' I told Cramer of having had Waldine Peckham put out the word that someone wanted to buy the sketch, no questions asked. 'Where did you find it?' I asked.

'In St. James's gallery, along with everything else. Carlton Wells said it was his. Looks like your teacher stole your work.'

'I'm just glad to have it back without any more people seeing it.'

'By the way, Mrs. Fletcher, I told you there was an influential person pressing behind the scenes for me to cooperate with you and your theories.'

'That's right. You did.'

'Go ahead and shake his hand,' he said, nodding at Vaughan Buckley.

'You? I thought you didn't like my getting

270

involved.'

'I don't. Then again, I knew there's no way to dissuade you once you've set your mind to it. Besides, it will make a good plot for your next bestseller.'

*   *   *

The next morning I stood next to my luggage on the porch of Scott's Inn. With me were Vaughan and Olga Buckley. A cadre of press was kept at a distance by two patrolmen assigned the task by their chief. Fred Mayer leaned against his taxi, the rear door open.

'Sure we can't convince you to stay longer?' Olga asked.

'I'd love to, Olga, but it's time for me to get back home.'

'Any more art lessons on the horizon?' Vaughan asked.

'No. It's back to my word processor, not my easel. I'm a writer, not a painter.'

'Can't say that I'm disappointed to hear that, Jess,' said Vaughan. 'That's where you belong, in front of a word processor. Leave the painting to Michelangelo and Renoir and Caravaggio.'

'I will. Thanks for everything. I'll be in touch.'

I got into Mayer's aging taxi. Once the doors were closed, I said, 'All set?'

'Certainly am. The missus is thrilled. Calls it

a second honeymoon.'

I smiled. 'Make it whatever you want it to be. Are you sure I'll like Gurney's Inn?'

'Never heard anybody say they didn't, Mrs. Fletcher.'

We picked up Mayer's wife, Carol, a lovely, kind woman, and headed east to Montauk, Long Island. My deal with her husband was simple: I wanted three days of total and secluded relaxation in some luxurious resort in the Hamptons. In return for his silence about my destination and for driving me there, I would foot the bill for a three-day vacation for him and his wife. He chose Gurney's Inn, and I didn't debate his choice. He hadn't steered me wrong yet.

I spent the three days in a cottage overlooking the Atlantic Ocean. The resort offered a dazzling array of spa services— aerobic beach walks, a daily cardiovascular fitness class, and such exotic therapies as 'marinotherapeutic' treatments (using seawater and seaweed), 'thalasso' therapy in which powerful underwater jets massage the body, and 'Dead Sea Salt Glow,' dead skin cells washed away in salt baths. I avoided the spa meals, opting instead to take all my meals in a lovely on-site restaurant, the Sea Grill, right on the beach.

Most of the time I painted. I set up the easel just outside my door and tried to capture the stunning beauty of the ocean. Fred Mayer had stopped in an art supply shop on the way to Gurney's, where I stocked up on everything I needed. The only thing I couldn't buy, of course, was artistic talent. But I wasn't about to be deterred by that. I would do my best.

It was one of the nicest three-day respites I'd ever experienced.

*　　*　　*

Four days later I was home in Cabot Cove. My friends, Dr. Seth Hazlitt and Sheriff Mort Metzger, threw me a welcome-home party at my home a week later. One of the guests was a local artist, John Leito, who was developing a solid reputation in galleries beyond Cabot Cove.

'Interesting work,' he said, referring to a seascape I'd just had framed, and had hung the day of the party. 'It's not signed.'

'Just one of many unsung artists,' I said. 'I think it's a view of the ocean from a resort in Montauk. That's on Long Island, on the far eastern end. It appealed to me.'

'The best reason for buying art,' he said.

He also paused at the other new painting hanging in my home.

'Now, that really interests me,' he said. 'So bold, so free. It reminds me of—' He clicked his fingers as he tried to come up with the name. 'Ah, Leopold. Joshua Leopold. Died young.'

'I wouldn't know,' I said. 'I bought it at a garage sale in the Hamptons for five dollars. Probably worth exactly that.'

'Unless it's a Leopold.'

'Unlikely. But if it is, I won't sell it. It has a certain nostalgic value to me. More lasagna, John? Better get it before Mort and Seth finish it off.'